"I can't tha
Sarah whis

He searched her face for a moment. She found herself breathless, waiting for...something.

"What are friends for?" he muttered and took a step back.

Sarah's eyes widened. Whatever she'd been waiting for, it wasn't that. Sighing disappointedly, she saw the dim lights of a buggy topping a hill in the distance.

"Oh dear! I forgot to tell my siblings I had a ride home already."

"Looks like they figured it out. Or saw you leave."

Sarah worried her lower lip. "Still, I'm usually not so...irresponsible."

Gideon swung back to face her. "Do you always have to be responsible, Sarah?"

"Of course! It's very import...import..." She stammered under the intensity of his gaze. "Responsibility is a *gut* thing, isn't it?"

"I don't know." Gideon's voice softened suddenly. "This is pretty irresponsible and it still seems like a pretty *gut* thing to me..."

Publishers Weekly bestselling author **Jocelyn McClay** grew up on an Iowa farm, ultimately pursuing a degree in agriculture. She met her husband while weight lifting in a small town—he "spotted" her. After thirty years in business management, they moved to an acreage in southeastern Missouri to be closer to family when their oldest of three daughters made them grandparents. When not writing, she keeps busy grandparenting, hiking, biking, gardening, quilting, knitting and substitute teaching.

Books by Jocelyn McClay

Love Inspired

The Amish Bachelor's Choice
Amish Reckoning
Her Forbidden Amish Love
Their Surprise Amish Marriage
Their Unpredictable Path
Her Unlikely Amish Protector
The Amish Spinster's Dilemma
Her Scandalous Amish Secret
Their Surprise Amish Reunion
Their Impossible Amish Match
Her Amish Christmas Wish

Visit the Author Profile page at LoveInspired.com.

HER AMISH CHRISTMAS WISH

JOCELYN McCLAY

If you purchased this book without a cover you should be aware that this book is stolen property. It was reported as "unsold and destroyed" to the publisher, and neither the author nor the publisher has received any payment for this "stripped book."

Recycling programs for this product may not exist in your area.

ISBN-13: 978-1-335-62126-9

Her Amish Christmas Wish

Copyright © 2025 by Jocelyn Ord

All rights reserved. No part of this book may be used or reproduced in any manner whatsoever without written permission.

Without limiting the author's and publisher's exclusive rights, any unauthorized use of this publication to train generative artificial intelligence (AI) technologies is expressly prohibited.

This is a work of fiction. Names, characters, places and incidents are either the product of the author's imagination or are used fictitiously. Any resemblance to actual persons, living or dead, businesses, companies, events or locales is entirely coincidental.

For questions and comments about the quality of this book, please contact us at CustomerService@Harlequin.com.

® is a trademark of Harlequin Enterprises ULC.

Love Inspired
22 Adelaide St. West, 41st Floor
Toronto, Ontario M5H 4E3, Canada
www.LoveInspired.com

HarperCollins Publishers
Macken House, 39/40 Mayor Street Upper,
Dublin 1, D01 C9W8, Ireland
www.HarperCollins.com

Printed in Lithuania

And Ruth said, Intreat me not to leave thee, or to return from following after thee: for whither thou goest, I will go; and where thou lodgest, I will lodge: thy people shall be my people, and thy God my God.
—*Ruth* 1:16

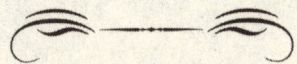

First and foremost, I thank God for the opportunity and answered prayers. Thanks to John for his experience with a planer, and Joe, paramedic extraordinaire. Lorelle, Misti and Ursula, I treasure your insights and encouragement. To my family, love you dearly. I couldn't have done this without you.

Chapter One

He loved this community.

That was why it was going to be so hard to leave it.

Gideon Schrock drew in a deep breath as he gazed over the farmyard, one dotted with small clusters of men visiting, all similarly dressed in white shirts, black pants, black vests and, in deference to the turn to autumn in Wisconsin, collarless black jackets. Gideon's lips twitched. They looked like a flock of crows. His budding smile froze and he swallowed hard. They were his crows, his flock. At least for now. Until he left.

He exhaled in a quiet gust. He had things to do before then. Things that weighed on him like an anvil on his chest. Someone...he grimaced, *several* someones to tell. He drew in another breath. But not now. Not when Church Sunday afternoons were meant for community.

His gaze drifted to the big white farmhouse, home of this week's host family. He pressed a faint smile into service, willing his troubled thoughts to follow the action. There was always something amusing or distracting in the world. He found it on the porch.

Whereas in the bird kingdom the males had brighter plumage, his flock was the opposite. Knots of women gathered on the porch or were interspersed throughout the yard.

They were dressed more colorfully than the black-garbed men, with calf-length dresses in solid blues and purples, a few greens, visible beneath capes and aprons.

The pleasant hum of conversations was occasionally accompanied by a distant moo from the black-and-white Holstein cows that dotted a far hill. Or a neigh from one of the many horses, currently unhitched from buggies that were lined like dominoes in a nearby, cropped hayfield.

His wandering gaze sharpened on two men leaning against the white rail fence. Their hair, blond like his— though they sported beards where he did not—contrasted with the mostly brown horses that waited slouch-hipped inside the fence or tied to the rail. His brothers were deep in discussion. Samuel, the local horse trader, would probably be talking about horses. His oldest brother, Malachi... Gideon rubbed an absent hand across his chest where his steady heartbeat abruptly escalated like an unbroken horse when a saddle was tossed onto his back.

Malachi would be talking about his business, Schrock Brothers Furniture. Gideon's pulse surged again. The business *he* was the brother in. The business he was leaving. As soon as he worked up the courage to tell Malachi.

It wasn't that he was unhappy working for his brother. Gideon licked dry lips at the self-lie. *Ach*, actually, he was, though he felt guilty acknowledging it. His brother was a *gut* boss. A fair boss. One who'd done an impressive job growing the business in the years since they'd moved to Miller's Creek. Malachi was fulfilling his dream.

But his brother's dream wasn't Gideon's dream.

He straightened his shoulders. He wasn't without ambition. His just didn't involve lathing table legs and dovetailing desk drawers forever. Or calculating how many screws and board feet were necessary to do so in commercial quantities. But his brother would be hurt to hear that, and once something was said, it couldn't be unsaid. It would always be there between them.

"You all right there, Gideon?"

Gideon whipped his attention back to the small circle of young men he was included in. Adept at hiding his thoughts, he gave the speaker a lazy smile as he dropped his hand. "*Ja,* Ben," he assured his friend and coworker. "Just wondering when was the last time I washed my shirt and if it was clean enough to allow me to remove my coat."

The surrounding men chuckled.

"I remember those days." Ben's brother Aaron reminisced. "That in itself was almost worth getting married."

"I don't know. As you chose so unwisely, marrying my sister, I think doing my own laundry, even hanging it out on the line, might be preferable."

Aaron grinned at Gideon's retort as another spurt of laughter rippled through the circle. "I'm surprised you still have to do your own wash. With all those single women constantly wearing a path to your door carrying their covered dishes, surely one has made an effort to take on your laundry as well?"

Gideon scratched his beardless chin, which identified him as being an unmarried man. "Now, that does sounds tempting. Maybe the way to a man's heart is not through his stomach but through the washing machine and clothesline. Though I do admit a casserole and a peach pie definitely win points on the journey."

"So who's the one with the most points?" Daniel Glick, husband of less than a year himself, entered the collective teasing. Gideon wasn't surprised at the man's interest in anything food-related. Daniel, along with his new wife, Rebecca, ran the Dew Drop, the primary restaurant in town.

"Why? You looking for another cook?" he countered, skilled at deflecting the current topic. Twenty-three and considered a good catch—whether because of his steady job or the blue eyes he'd once overheard a few young women giggling over—Gideon was an old hand at being ribbed about his single status.

If he was leaving—though he retained his smile, Gideon tightened his lips—*and he was*, at least when he left he wouldn't be pulling a young wife away from her family. It was one of the reasons he hadn't seriously searched for a bride. But not seriously searching didn't mean he didn't enjoy the efforts of the numerous young women trying to change his mind.

Before Daniel could respond, a blue-and-white ball dropped into the center of their loose circle. Aaron grabbed it before it bounced away.

"Sorry about that!" Sarah Raber dashed over to retrieve it. She gave Aaron, her older brother, a gentle jab in the ribs when he handed her the ball. "Of course, if you old men had any reflexes, you could have hit it back to us."

"Ouch. If you had any skill, you could've kept it in bounds."

Gideon's teasing drew Sarah's gaze. "What's your excuse? Why aren't you playing volleyball instead of hanging out here with these old men?"

Having known her almost as long as he'd known Ben, Gideon was used to her banter.

"Maybe I was just scouting to see which team was worth joining."

"Mine. But you'd have to be a *gut* player to get on it." She gave him a sympathetic smile. "So I can see why you're still on the sidelines." Her smile morphing instantly into a cheeky grin, Sarah departed as abruptly as she'd arrived.

Her *kapp* bounced on top of her dark hair as she jogged back to the court, leaving Gideon the recipient of several snickers.

"So, does Sarah ever bring you food?"

"*Nee*, Sarah doesn't like to cook." Ben saved Gideon from responding to Daniel's amused query.

"And after having had to eat what she's made, we don't like her to either."

Though Aaron's words were glib, both his and his brother's eyes didn't match their easy smiles as their gazes followed their sister.

Though his own brow puckered at their expressions, Gideon snorted. Now, that would be something. He and Sarah. Everyone seemed to think they were a couple. But they weren't. Not that he didn't like her. He liked Sarah quite well. She was fun. Quick-witted, hardworking. A lot of *gut* qualities.

But a sweetheart? Certainly not. Not for him, at least. It would be like dating a sister.

He'd given Sarah a look—a long one—when, at age eighteen, he'd joined Malachi and Samuel and moved to the Miller's Creek, Wisconsin, district. Then he'd looked at Ben and decided he wanted his new coworker's friendship more. Flirting with the man's barely fourteen-year-old sister wouldn't go far in winning it. So, relegating Sarah to the role of a younger sister, he'd fallen into an easy relationship with her, more so because of how much he missed the sisters he'd left back in Ohio.

Gideon watched as Sarah took her place on the makeshift court's trampled grass and tossed the ball back to the server. Come to think of it, during the numerous times he'd been over to the Raber house to visit Ben—and mooch a meal—before his friend had married, Sarah had never been the cook.

She'd done many other things, cleaning, laundry, taking

care of younger siblings—particularly Anne—but she'd never done the cooking. It was always her *mamm* or one of the younger Raber girls. His gaze narrowed. Maybe she couldn't cook. Which was odd, as most Amish girls learned the skill at a young age. If so, it would be about the only thing he could think of that Sarah couldn't do. She was extremely capable.

As was he.

He just had to keep reminding himself of that. It was a bit hard to remember when always trailing in the shadows of his talented brothers, but he'd finally started on his own journey. If not yet by foot, at least by letter. He inhaled sharply, earning himself another questioning side-eye from Ben. Gideon smiled and shook his head slightly. To distract from any more quizzical glances, Gideon launched into an embellished tale, much to the amusement of the surrounding men, of an appealing-looking gift of an apple pie, one which was more peeling than pie upon closer inspection.

Sarah's sigh was as heavy as her weighted shoulders as she strode from the buggy and its occupant. What was she going to do about Anne? She grimaced. Her *mamm* and *daed* reassured her it wasn't her problem. That Anne would come around. They weren't concerned. She should follow their example. The *Biewel* said to *cast thy burden upon the Lord and he shall sustain thee.*

But Sarah knew she had a problem when it came to casting. Particularly when related to Anne.

At least her new job paid well. Better than her old one. That would help with the bills. Again, ones her folks said weren't her problem. Sarah clenched her hands. But they were. And she would keep working to cover existing bills and any new ones incurred from needed future surgeries. She couldn't have her family or the community pay for something she was responsible for. She'd make it right. Wincing, Sarah jerked to a halt. That was impossible. It would never be right—but she'd make it as right as she could. She blew out a long breath before striding on.

Money wasn't the only cost. To earn it, she needed to work, and to work as a young Amish woman, she needed to stay single. Newly married women established homes. They started their families. Sarah bit her lower lip as she glanced in the direction of the house's wide porch. All her buddy bunch friends were there, chatting with the other married women of the district. Her buddy bunch. They'd been baptized together. Baptism was a requirement before getting married and they'd all known they wanted to join the church, marry and stay together in the Amish community.

And *they* were. All married now. While she, whom everyone had assumed would marry first as she had always been the one with a beau—many of them her friends' now-husbands—was still single.

Her steps slowed as she watched them interact, smiling, occasionally bursting into laughter. Was her buddy bunch getting together without her? One by one, as they'd married, they'd stopped going to singings, as those were for the single folks. These were the friends Sarah had expected to have cookie and cleaning frolics with. Rotate quilting parties in their homes. They were now attending gatherings with their husbands and other young married couples. And she was…left out. Feeling a bit hollow, Sarah sniffed, recalling how last time she'd gotten together with those friends, the talk had all been about marriage and youngsters. She'd had little to contribute to the conversations, other than to mutely wish she was a young wife as well.

Her friend Grace's recent marriage might have been the last wedding she'd attended, but there'd been other weddings.

Ones of girls a few years behind Sarah when they'd attended school. Even they were moving on. Leaving her behind.

At least the younger unmarried girls looked up to her. Included her. Several had been involved in the recently ended volleyball game. But it wasn't the same. Sarah felt like an old hen in a chicken run full of pullets.

As she approached the volleyball court, her gaze swept its fringes and landed on a woman standing on the sideline with a few other players. The blonde was young, but not as young as the others. And still unmarried. Otherwise she wouldn't have been hired as the new schoolteacher to replace Grace.

As they'd filed in to church with the other single women this morning, Sarah had entered alongside Dorothy and sat with her on the backless bench. They'd visited in the brief moments allowed during the service and then afterward, over sandwiches of church spread, before Sarah had been called away to join a volleyball game. With another quick glance at the chummy groups on the porch, Sarah veered in the direction of the blonde. The schoolteacher, new to the area, was nice and, more importantly, seemed as interested in finding a friend as Sarah was.

Her spirits lifted when Dorothy greeted her with a big smile. "Sarah, am I glad to see you. So many new faces and names." She pressed her palms to her cheeks. "I don't know how I'll remember them all."

"I'm sure the school board president will arrange some type of gathering for you to get to know the students' parents. He normally tries to do that before school starts. But things were in a little upheaval when Grace, the previous teacher, got married unexpectedly this summer."

"That's all right. I'll get to know names soon enough, but right now, it's a little overwhelming."

"As long as you don't forget mine." A man around their age appeared at Dorothy's elbow, his flat-brimmed straw hat perched rakishly on his dark hair.

Sarah snorted. "As if anyone could, Josiah. You're like a noxious weed that's difficult to eliminate from a pasture." She tipped her head in his direction. "Dorothy, this is Josiah Lapp. His *daed* has one of the large dairy farms in the community." Sarah's lips slanted as she watched her new friend blush faintly. Dorothy obviously thought Josiah was cute. *Ach*, he was. And he knew it.

"Careful. He's a flirt." Sarah eyed Josiah, who looked far from wounded at the warning. "But he is fun, which makes him hard not to like," she conceded. "Are you recruiting, Josiah?"

"I don't need to recruit. Folks flock to join me."

She propped her hands on her hips and made a production of looking about their small group, currently consisting of him, her, Dorothy and a few younger girls. "I don't see a flock. All I see is a single goose."

"I'll have a team gathered up before you do. And beat you with it too." He flashed a white-toothed smile at Dorothy. "I just wanted to be sure to first enlist this new talent."

Sarah rolled her eyes at the blonde with an "I told you so" look. "You're on. Ten minutes?"

"Challenge accepted." He dipped his head toward Dorothy. "My team, remember." With a parting wink, he headed for a group of *youngies* seated at a nearby picnic table.

"Can we be on your team, Sarah?"

"For sure and certain," Sarah turned to the younger girls with a smile. "But you better go find us one." The two dashed off to do some recruiting of their own.

"You're right. He is quite the flirt."

Sarah was glad Dorothy seemed to have some sense, although the woman's cheeks were still more than a tad pink. She raised her eyebrows, though, at the woman's next words.

"He's one of the many attractive men you have in your district."

Cocking her head, Sarah glanced at the community's young men, scattered in small clusters, and considered those she'd grown up with from an outsider's view. Attractive? She supposed so, though most of the appealing ones had already married her friends. She shrugged. She'd probably be checking out the single men if she was new in a district as well.

"Like him." Dorothy nodded toward someone over Sarah's shoulder. "I'm assuming he's single. No beard and sitting earlier along the church bench with Josiah. He...stands out." Her blush bloomed again.

Sarah turned to see who her new friend was looking at. The only single man in that direction was the one her two recruiters were currently talking to. She frowned at the sudden pang in her stomach. *I should've had more than just a church spread sandwich for dinner if I was going to play volleyball all afternoon.* She ignored the odd ache. "That's Gideon. Gideon Schrock. He works at his *bruder*'s furniture shop." She smiled faintly. *As do I now.*

"Is he...?" Dorothy raised an eyebrow. Color marched farther up her cheeks.

Sarah's smile melted like ice cream in July. The unspoken word was *available*. Another pang, more resonating this time, shot through her stomach. She glanced toward Dorothy, taking in her delicate features, big blue eyes, blond hair neatly pulled back under a pristine *kapp*.

She cleared her throat. "As far as I know. Gideon isn't one to kiss and tell. Although he is one to kiss," she muttered. Sarah grimaced. "Or so say those who do tell, at least."

What was the matter with her? One sandwich had always been enough before on Church Sundays. Maybe it wasn't hunger? Maybe it was that she didn't like discussing Gideon—available Gideon—with a pretty, *and interested*, newcomer? Nonsense. She fixed a smile back on her face. Dorothy was going to be a good friend. Just like Gideon was. And that was all he was.

Once upon a time, she'd hoped, like many other girls in the surrounding communities still did, that he'd be something more. But Gideon was like the particularly slippery fish in a local pond that everyone wanted to catch. No matter what lures were thrown at him, he managed to evade them.

Her eyes narrowed on the man currently smiling down at her younger teammates. Dorothy was right. Gideon was attractive. All the Schrock brothers were. When the three had first moved into town several years ago, the question circulating among the district's young single women of "Which Schrock brother do you like?" was as common as *"Wie ghets?"*—with the questioner far more interested in the answer on the Schrocks than the courteous "How is it going?" for a friend.

For her, it had been Gideon. All the girls had been jealous when he'd become Ben's *gut* friend and began spending a lot of time at her home. Though she did her best to attract and attach his interest, it hadn't taken her long to realize he was solely there for Ben's company and her *mamm*'s cooking. He'd treated her like a little sister. Knowing she'd have to work for years to pay accumulating bills, Sarah had comfortably settled into the role instead of one that, though exciting, was impossible, then and now. She was glad he'd responded as he had, as over the years, she and Gideon had become *gut* friends too. They laughed at folks' notions they were anything beyond that.

Despite her teasing earlier this afternoon, he was a *gut* volleyball player. Sarah's lips twitched at the two young women planted in front of Gideon. They wouldn't have much success. He didn't participate often with the *youngies* in their *rumspringa*. Like her, most of his friends were married. That wasn't dissuading the two girls, though.

She raised an eyebrow as Gideon shed his collarless *mutza* jacket and hung it over the fence before heading in her direction. Maybe she shouldn't be surprised. Gideon had a soft spot for the youth. The two girls—flushed with their success—dashed to recruit a few of the younger men. Sarah turned back to Dorothy, but the schoolteacher's attention was diverted by the arrival of Josiah and his assembled team.

She grinned at Gideon as he approached. "We had to scramble to gather a team, so I guess if we have to, we'll take you."

"I'll try not to let you down."

When he responded with a wink and crooked smile of his own, Sarah's eyes briefly widened. It remained to be seen if Dorothy was a good teacher. But the newcomer was a good judge of other things. Sarah had forgotten what an attractive man Gideon was.

"Out!"

"How can you say that, Josiah? It almost bounced off your foot."

"My foot was on the line."

"We need a line judge. One shouldn't be both a player and a judge. At least *you* shouldn't."

Gideon stifled a snort. Sarah had propped hands on her slender hips and glared through the volleyball net as Josiah retrieved the blue-and-white ball from where it had rolled to a stop behind a buggy wheel. The blonde girl beside him—the new schoolteacher, according to what he'd learned in murmured conversation during church—covered her mouth with one hand as she giggled.

"You're just afraid that you might get beat this time." Josiah tossed the ball behind him to where Noah Reihl stood at the back of the grassy court.

"Not if I can help it." Sarah, playing a row ahead of him, braced for the serve.

The ball lofted over the net, descending between the front and back row. Gideon bolted forward, watching the ball to time a jump to spike it back. In his peripheral vision, he saw Sarah rapidly backpedaling. Before he could dodge, they collided.

Gideon instinctively wrapped his arms around Sarah to prevent her from falling. Jerking her against his chest, he staggered a few steps to avoid tumbling to the ground himself. Though he managed to keep his feet, his senses continued to tumble. Soft, warm flesh filled his arms, pressing against him from shoulder to toes. His sharp inhalation drew in the scent of flowers. Honeysuckle? Lilac? Whatever it was came from the silky strands of dark hair that clung to his lips where his mouth was pressed against her forehead. He reflexively tightened his arms around her as he drew in another breath.

Sarah's elbows were caught between them. She leaned back, lifting her head from where it was tucked into his shoulder. Gideon ran a quick tongue over his lips to stop their tingling as the strands pulled free. He was bombarded with an avalanche of impressions. To his shock, none of them were brotherly.

Chapter Two

"Are you all right?" He was breathless, as if he'd been running. But the only thing racing was his heart. Right now, Gideon was so bemused he didn't think he could take a step if he had to.

Sarah looked up at him and slowly exhaled. *"Ja."* Her breath wafted over his face in a sweet, warm rush. "Did we get it?"

Gideon blinked. Had he ever seen her this close up? Seen that her eyes were the deep color of blueberries and the lashes that fringed them were as long and lush as a pasture in spring? "Get what?"

The brow above her striking eyes knit with impatience. "The ball. Did we get the ball over the net?"

Gideon tore his gaze from her face and looked around vaguely. "I...don't know."

Sarah leaned back as far as his embrace would allow, to eye him doubtfully. "Are *you* all right?" She reached up to touch where her *kapp* was flattened against her hair. "Did we hit heads? You're acting a bit strange."

He *was* feeling a bit strange. Gideon flexed his hands briefly where they rested at her waist before sliding them a safe distance down her arms as he set her away from him.

Maybe they did hit heads. Maybe that explained his...befuddlement.

Josiah's challenging hoot from the far side of the net advised the result of the play. With a faint grimace at the lost point, Sarah stepped back, shook out her skirt and readjusted the hairpins holding her *kapp* as she returned to the front row. If the collision had affected her beyond wrinkling her clothes, it didn't show.

But for him... Gideon muffed his serving opportunity, sending the ball winging past the back boundary. His teammates, including Sarah, all turned to give him a quizzical look. He never missed a serve. If he played, he was usually a guarantee for several points. But not today. Today, he...well, his mind wasn't on the game, much less his serve. Sarah kept pacing on the trampled grass in front of him. When he'd brought his hand back to serve, the wind tugged her blue dress high enough to reveal slender calves and dainty ankles above her bare feet. The view distracted him. He was lucky his serve didn't fly into the midst of the lounging horses and spook them.

The wind might have fluttered the other girls' dresses, revealing other calves and ankles, but Gideon didn't notice them. He hadn't previously noticed Sarah's. But now, as she bounced on her toes preparing for Josiah's serve, their trimness drew his gaze like a magnet. He glanced up when she returned the ball in time to see it skim over the frayed net, directly at the new schoolteacher. The blonde squeaked and jerked her arms up as much in defense as to return the volley. The ball careened off her uplifted hands and shot out of bounds.

"That's game!" crowed one of the young men on his team. The schoolteacher cringed and ducked her head.

"That's all right. You'll probably get us next time."

Gideon was just relieved the game was over. The blonde looked up to reward his encouragement with a grateful smile.

Sarah slipped under the net and patted the teacher on the shoulder. "All you need to do is get Josiah off your team," she spoke loudly enough to ensure the approaching team captain heard.

"We *will* get you next time, Sarah. For sure and certain," Josiah countered before consoling the blonde himself.

Sarah waved his response away as she headed off the court. Gideon's eyes narrowed. Was she limping? He trailed slowly after her, intermittently stopped by other *youngies* to whom he gave brief nods and smiles while surreptitiously watching Sarah walk to a lone buggy parked nearby. *Ja*, she was. Once she got away from the eyes of others. He wouldn't have noticed if he hadn't been paying close attention. Increasing his pace, he caught up with her when she reached the buggy.

"Are you limping?"

"*Ja*. I think you stepped on me." At his wince, Sarah smiled. "Afraid you injured me and I can't start work for your *bruder* tomorrow?"

"We're a furniture business. There're plenty of chairs in the showroom. Malachi won't care if you sit for a bit."

Sarah frowned at him. "*I* would. I intend to do a *gut* job and that doesn't include sitting down at work."

Gideon's stomach twisted at the prospect of having hurt her. He rubbed a hand across the back of his neck as he stared at her bare foot. At least now he had an excuse. "I'm not as heavy as one of your *daed*'s Belgians. Or maybe not quite as heavy. But I am shod." He lifted one booted foot. "Can I take a look at it?"

Without waiting for her response, he sank onto his

haunches for a closer examination of her limb. Had it swelled since he'd, er, checked her out earlier? He ran a critical gaze comparing the top of her right foot to her left. Maybe a bit puffier. Did he dare run his fingers over it? He'd done so with a number of horse fetlocks to identify issues when the animal favored a foot. He'd know better by feel if it was swelling. But the thought of touching Sarah's foot now had him curling his fingers into his palm. Gideon frowned. What if it was fractured? With a long inhalation, he tentatively reached for her foot, only to have it disappear with a flurry of her full blue skirt as she whisked her leg behind the wheel's wooden spokes.

Sarah narrowed her eyes at him. "You might not be a Belgian, but neither are you a veterinarian or a farrier, so keep your hands off my leg."

Gideon squinted up at her. "How badly do you hurt?"

She looked away, pressing her lips together. "It'll pass," she finally muttered. "I'll be fine for work tomorrow."

Gideon stood, leaned an elbow on the buggy's wooden wheel and moved to a safer topic. "Does your determination to not sit at work include in the office?" Turning his head toward the open window of the buggy, he raised his voice. "What do you think, Anne? How long will your stubborn sister stand if she is working on numbers? As she plans to stay standing, would a chalkboard installed in the office make it easier for her to jot down the receipts? That might make it pretty hard if Malachi wanted to take the day's bookwork home to go over with his wife."

"I don't know," a childish voice floated out the window. "She's pretty stubborn."

Gideon eyed Sarah. "I've discovered that." He knew what her reaction would be to *his* newly discovered impressions. If he was fool enough to act on them, they'd probably get the same treatment as her sore foot. Disregarded, rapidly dismissed or maybe even kicked, sore foot notwithstanding, for his lunacy. Gideon twisted his lips. Best to follow her example with her foot pain and ignore these odd twinges until they went away. And hope he recovered without incident and without his work being affected.

The buggy door creaked as he opened it to reveal a frail young girl sitting on the dark leather seat. Even in the pleasantness of the fall day, a worn patchwork quilt was spread over her lap. Though the little one smiled at the sight of him, when the sunlight touched her, she flipped a corner of the quilt up to cover her neck and buried her hands underneath it.

Gideon gave Anne a lazy grin. "I imagine things ought to be getting pretty settled at the school, now that they've got a new schoolteacher hired and Grace can go back to being a newly wedded wife. I guess that means you'll be writing on a chalkboard soon too."

Anne's smile fell like a heavy bale dropped from a hayloft.

Sarah's stomach plunged at the same speed Anne's smile did. She hissed in a breath and braced herself.

"I'm not going."

She winced. Her younger sister's flat statement pained her more than any injury to her own extremities did. "Anne. We don't have to talk about this here," she murmured.

"It doesn't matter where we talk about it. I'm not going to school."

Frowning, Sarah shot a glance at their audience. Though the tension emanating from inside the buggy regarding the ongoing argument climbed as high as the pressure in a cooker in canning season, Gideon wore an easy smile on his face.

He idly scratched his cheek. "I didn't want to start school either when it was time to go." Sarah's glance sharpened into a "you're not helping" glare.

He continued, ignoring her. "But at the time, I missed my older *brieder* who were already going. Though for the life of me now, I don't know why."

Sarah rolled her eyes. Despite Gideon's jibe, she knew he'd do anything for his brothers.

He leaned closer to Anne and raised an eyebrow. "They talked of something called 'recess', which sounded pretty interesting. Then they started speaking the *Englisch* they were learning in school around me, using it as a secret code so I couldn't understand them. And they were learning how to do things with numbers that I couldn't do. Addition and subtraction with things around the farm to show how smart they were. If we had this much hay in the loft and needed to throw down this much every day, how many days of hay were in the loft?" He snorted. "I finally decided I wanted to go to school too, just to show them I was smarter than they were."

Anne eyed him skeptically. "And were you?"

Gideon grinned. "I'm still working on that. But I did learn *Englisch* and I did learn my numbers. And playing ball at recess was a lot of fun."

Anne's brow puckered. She was quiet a moment. "That's nice," she finally allowed. "But I'm still not going. They'll make…" Pressing her lips together, she tucked her chin into the top of the quilt. "I'm not going."

"If you don't start now, you'll be a year behind in finishing school at eighth grade," Sarah said, trying a new argument. "That might not seem like much now, but it might when your friends leave and you're still there." *Or when they all marry and leave you behind.* She swallowed against the thickness in her throat.

"I don't have friends."

"Oh, Anne. You do. Or you will." If she'd only allow herself to. She'd spent so much time in the hospital and then at home, recovering. Then they couldn't let her outside due to risk of infection, among other things. So she'd gotten comfortable staying away from others. Sarah pressed a hand against her roiling stomach. Just another thing she was responsible for.

"I know you'll make friends when the other *kinner* get to know you." *When you let them get to know you.* "You'll find some friends for life. A buddy bunch." Sarah firmed her lips so they didn't tremble at the reminder her bunch was moving on without her. "You'll wear the same colors to singings and other outings. Go to frolics and for buggy rides together."

Anne mutely shook her head and burrowed her chin deeper into the quilt.

Sarah grimaced. The school board, understanding the situation, had given Anne a pass for not attending last year. But they felt strongly about educating the district's youth in the shortened years the Amish had worked out with the government—taking it all the way to the Supreme Court— decades ago. At some point, Anne needed to begin her formal education. Sarah's stomach churned further at the thought of her sister not learning to read or decipher. The prospect of Anne being miserable for the majority of the day while she reluctantly sat in school didn't help either.

Sighing, she leaned back from the buggy. Gideon followed suit and quietly shut the door.

* * *

When Sarah took a few steps away from the buggy, Gideon, his frowning gaze on her troubled face, joined her. His eyes widened at his compelling urge to wrap his arms around her and soothe her obvious worries. To refrain from the unexpected—and unwanted—yearning, he folded them across his chest.

Pivoting so her back was to the conveyance, Sarah tipped her head toward him and muttered, "Although a bit reluctant, she seemed fine with it early this summer. Then all of a sudden, she determined she wasn't going. We can't talk her into it. My folks and I thought, as we knew Grace was only teaching until they got a new teacher hired and moved in, that we'd wait until everything was settled. Less change for Anne."

Inhaling the fresh, sweet scent of her that had so beguiled him earlier—he was almost certain it was honeysuckle—Gideon briefly lost track of the conversation. He straightened, putting a fraction of space between them, took a few deep breaths of less tantalizing air and caught her final words.

"But now that Dorothy is here..." Gideon followed her gaze to the young blond woman in a cluster of other *youngies*.

Sarah hunched a shoulder. "She still refuses to go. And you called me the stubborn one."

He forced himself to focus on the topic and not the woman beside him. Having been a friend of the Rabers for years, he knew of Anne's struggles but also recognized what a bright child she was. "Is she afraid of the school work?"

Sarah shook her head. "I don't think so. She likes to

learn. She's just so shy. Because of..." She grimaced. "You know."

He frowned. "But she's grown up with the *kinner* that she'll be attending school with."

"She's never made an effort to get to know them. For quite some time, she couldn't go out, so now she doesn't generally like to play with others. Just keeps to herself. She did try last Church Sunday. I was hopeful, but she came home insisting she wasn't going to do that again and didn't want to go to school." Sarah worried her lower lip. "I don't know what to do."

Gideon had no answer. No answer either to the consistent and unsettling impulse to comfort her. He found himself gently squeezing her shoulder in reassurance before realizing he'd unfolded his arms. He dropped his hand as if the fabric of her dress—and the slender but firm feel of the shoulder beneath it—burned his palm.

He cleared his throat. "Let me know if there's anything I can do to help." The offer earned him a vague smile. He wanted to expand it. "How's the foot? Do I need to drag an ottoman into the office for you tomorrow?"

Sarah wrinkled her nose as, standing on one foot, she flexed her foot experimentally. Gideon fought the impulse to look at her newly discovered ankles and kept his gaze on her face. "*Nee*. It's fine."

He nodded toward the court where teams were being organized. "Fine enough to play another game?"

She smiled but shook her head. "I'll just keep Anne company for a while." Sarah slipped past him to climb into the buggy and pulled the door shut behind her.

Gideon rubbed a hand over his heart and scowled. Inhaling deeply, he caught just a tinge of her scent. Definitely honeysuckle. Must be her shampoo as Amish women didn't wear perfume. He scowled. He'd been around many single women but never before thought or cared about what they washed their hair with. Of all times to have noticed Sarah as anything other than, well, Sarah.

Surely the feeling would leave as abruptly as it arrived? He'd been around her for years. He'd never noticed...*ach*... that she'd grown up. Grown up or not, they'd been friends too long for his recent discovery to change anything. He pulled his shoulders back and pressed his lips together. He was leaving. Singly. Just as soon as he found the right moment to tell Malachi he was leaving the business.

With a last troubled look over his shoulder at the two inside the buggy, Gideon sauntered over to the group that currently included his older brother. The other men shifted to make room for him in their gathering as one of them called a greeting.

"Gideon. We were just talking about Malachi's purchase of the old warehouse down by the railway. What do you think of his plans to double the business?"

"Double? I'd say it's well more than triple. That warehouse is easily..."

Gideon didn't hear the men's collective responses through the roaring in his ears. His jaw sagged. He knew the warehouse. It was immense. He knew its rumored price. Also immense. His mouth closed with a click of teeth. He hadn't heard a word of the purchase from the one who should have told him. His gaze pinned his brother. Beneath the brim of his hat, Malachi's normally unflappable face was flushed above a knotted jaw. He gave Gideon a tight, albeit sheepish smile.

"Looks like we're expanding. *Gut* thing it's Schrock Brothers. I need you now more than ever, little brother."

Chapter Three

Malachi rubbed his hand over the back of his neck. "*Ach*, I've been meaning to tell you. Just haven't found the time." The gaze that flicked to their avid audience before returning to him told Gideon this wasn't the time either.

Gideon felt like he'd been kicked simultaneously in the stomach and the head by a horse—one shod with studded winter shoes. He bit the inside of his cheek to forestall a response he might later regret. When he had enough air— and almost enough control—to speak, it was through stiff lips. "I look forward to talking with you when you do." His voice sounded half an octave lower than normal. Aware of the surrounding interest, he forced a smile, though the look that drilled his brother burned with frustration. Frustration and...a surprising avalanche of hurt.

Malachi's gaze flickered. His chin dipped slightly in subtle acknowledgment. "That reminds me. Ruth wanted me to have you stop by before you left today. She had something she wanted to ask you. Maybe you'll be lucky and it'll be an invitation to supper."

Under the excuse of glancing around for his sister-in-law, Gideon schooled his expression to a milder one. Malachi's wife was nowhere in sight. "In that case, no time like the present. Especially when it might include a meal."

Leaving a chorus of chuckles behind them, he and Malachi fell into brisk step beside each other.

"I'm sorry," Malachi murmured when they were out of earshot. "I never would have wanted you to find out that way."

"What way *did* you want me to find out? The news has apparently had enough time to make its way around the Amish grapevine before finally reaching me." To Gideon's chagrin, dismay and bitterness soaked his response. He clenched his lips, along with his fists.

Malachi bowed his head. "You're right."

"You always say I'm part of the business, yet you've already bought this warehouse without saying anything to me?" The words tumbled out. Emotions, ones he couldn't—or wouldn't—find voice for, whirled even more turbulently. He jerked to a halt. "Does Samuel know?"

Malachi's wince revealed that while *he* hadn't been told, Malachi had shared the news with Gideon's other older brother. Planting his hands on his hips, Gideon quarter-turned away. He sucked in a deep breath to overcome the stabbing ache at being left out, the last one to know.

"He's not even part of the operation anymore."

Malachi cleared his throat as he tugged his broad-brimmed felt hat lower. "*Ach*, being an owner of a business, he understands expansion concerns…"

Gideon grimaced at the acknowledgment. He bit back a toxic retort. *Yet I'm the brother affected and you didn't tell me.* The words were equally noxious to swallow. His two older brothers had a particular bond he would never penetrate. Normally that didn't bother him. Much. Today, the exclusion burned like a hot poker.

Apparently he was easy to read as well. "I was wrong. If I told anyone—well, other than Ruth—it should have been you." Malachi reached up tentatively to squeeze Gideon's shoulder. "I'm sorry, little brother."

So was Gideon. Very sorry.

Malachi's hand was warm on his shoulder. *I'm not your "little brother" anymore. I'm almost as old as you were when you started your own business.* Gideon braced to jerk out of reach when into the quagmire of bitterness and dismay trickled a bit of guilt. He hadn't told Malachi of his own plans, ones which would also affect his brother's business.

Tension abruptly drained from his limbs. Regardless of when he'd found out about the new acquisition, how could he tell his brother—his boss—he was now leaving when Malachi needed him? And Malachi would. One of the reasons Gideon had delayed telling of his upcoming departure was that Schrock Brothers had been extremely busy, barely keeping up with the general growth Malachi had brought in the door and the seasonal surge as furniture shops ordered in for holiday sales.

But at least when he shared his news, his brother would be the *first* one in the district to know. Not the last, like he'd been.

Tamping down the impulse to wrench away, Gideon instead eased a step back. Malachi's hand dropped slowly to his side. Gideon began walking again. To where, he didn't know. The comment about Ruth had obviously been a cover to get them away from the group. Just as well. There was an ache in his stomach that had nothing to do with food. With no other destination in mind, he turned toward where he'd left his horse. His steps quickened at the prospect of heading home to lick his wounds.

Malachi again fell into step beside him. From a glimpse of his brother's face, it appeared Malachi's stomach felt similar to his. Gideon scowled. He didn't want to cause his brother grief. With a long, chest-emptying sigh, he recalled how Malachi had always been there for him, even when he was little. As a middle child in a large brood, Gideon had gotten a bit lost in the shuffle. Malachi had taught him many things, always with great patience. Had encouraged him. Included him. Even in this furniture business. At least until Gideon had realized he no longer wanted to be included.

So why was he fussing so much when he wasn't? It was a logical argument, but one his aching stomach—and heart—fought against.

The internal battle raged for several more brisk steps before he cleared his throat. "So...tell me about this new purchase." His voice, like his enthusiasm, was as tepid as a tea bag on its fifth use, but at least he got the words out.

Malachi shot him a glance. Gideon forced another smile, though a weak and twitchy one. It gained strength when Malachi's pinched expression eased and his *bruder* released a sigh rivaling Gideon's earlier one.

"With the growth in the business, both out of the showroom and in shipments to the furniture stores we've picked up, space has gotten tight, even for the staff we've got. It makes a challenge for us to keep up. We need to add more employees. I think the warehouse can remedy that, and also give us opportunities to expand into cabinetry."

Gideon's eyes widened, his smile disappearing.

Noting his reaction, Malachi hastened on. "Though I did just recently buy the warehouse, I have been thinking about this for some time. Madison isn't that far away and it's growing. The *Englisch* are moving farther out from it and building houses in the smaller surrounding towns. New houses need cabinetry. Our local Amish communities are growing as well. Both naturally with large families and by folks moving to Miller's Creek from in and out of state."

Gideon winced inwardly. True indeed. Their area was growing so much that it was difficult to find land, something a man needed to keep a horse and start a family. If he did find some, the price was sky high. It wasn't a factor for Gideon as he had his own place. But it would be for any children he might have.

More buggies and motorized vehicles concentrated in the area meant an increase in the possibility of an accident. The buggies and their occupants by far came out on the worse end. These were just some of the reasons he was ready to leave.

"New church districts are being established as original ones are outgrown. Men will be looking for jobs. We can provide them." Malachi lifted his hat and ran a rough hand through his hair. "But it will take some skill set development." His gaze cut to Gideon.

Ah. This was where he would come in. He'd be teaching new hires about furniture making. Gideon managed not to scowl. He supposed he could do all right with that. He was usually a pretty patient guy. Hopefully Malachi hired sharp enough employees that everyone could get up the learning curve without losing a finger. Working around their kind of tools could be dangerous. Even for experienced hands.

"With the new warehouse's truck docks, we can load out the cabinetry and furniture shipments more easily. Although we'd still use Amish mills for specialty lumber and some regular orders, the docks could handle lumber by *Englisch* truckload as well, keeping some supply chain costs down."

Normally even-keeled, Malachi fairly burst with enthusiasm as he continued. "There's even enough room on the new property to build a shed to handle everyone's horses. Now we're so cramped for space here we barely have room for Sarah's horse. The new warehouse is why I..." Apparently catching himself, Malachi frowned apologetically. "Why *we* hired Sarah. We'll move the actual production to the other site and revamp this location to be a full showroom. Maybe add some small booths for other local Amish artisans who don't have a shop in town. I should have talked to you about it before I signed the paperwork. Even before then. But it *is* a good business opportunity."

He smiled faintly. "You have always said you wonder why it's called 'Schrock Brothers' when all you do is make furniture, which, for sure and certain, you do very well. But you're an important part of the business and I need you now more than ever. I'm depending on you to manage things at the existing location. Supervise the operation there while I'm busy setting up the warehouse." He shook his head. "So much to do. Layout, equipment purchase and installation, power setup..." Even with the daunting prospect of the heavy workload, his brother's excitement was evident.

Gideon gritted his teeth. Training, he could do. Even accomplish it with everyone's digits still intact. But manage? Supervise anyone beyond himself? *Nee.* That was a role he'd never wanted.

His distress must've been evident, as Malachi reached toward him before curling his fingers into his palm and returning his hand to his side. "You're ready. Sarah can take care of the showroom and any of the work up front. I'll be stopping in." Malachi snorted softly. "Quite frequently probably, until I get an office established at the other building."

Gideon's jaw remained locked. Being ready didn't mean being willing.

Malachi rubbed a hand over his chin as they reached where Gideon's mare was tied along the fence with several other horses. "I know this is a conversation we should've had before. Long before. I'll keep you apprised from now on. It was just...*ach*, I was apprehensive about the thought of such a large expansion, about the expense, but it seemed like such a *gut* fit for the business." He smiled at Gideon. "And I knew you'd be there to help. I couldn't do it without you."

Gideon managed a wavering return smile as Malachi's gaze searched his face. Seemingly satisfied, his brother nodded. "I'll see you tomorrow morning, then. Briefly at least, as I'm meeting with Jonah Lapp at the warehouse to go over some things." Following a final smile accompanied by a penetrating gaze, Malachi pivoted to scan the farmyard before heading for a cluster of women that included his wife.

Gideon's smile dropped as soon as Malachi's back was turned. His brother had gotten as far as talking with a local carpenter but hadn't breathed a word to him? Another pang—a pitchfork in the gut—struck him at the knowledge of being left out until this late stage when everyone else had been informed. Even included.

His jerk freeing the lead rope from the post caused Jazz to fling up her head. Gideon was immediately contrite. It took a few gentle strokes on the mare's soft nose while she watched him warily for her to calm down. The soothing interaction helped settle him as well.

The ache that weighed on his shoulders wasn't about not being included in the initial decision-making. He grimaced. It was, after all, Malachi's business. His brother was the one who'd saved money to buy what was originally his wife's father's furniture business. He was the one who'd arranged the move up to Wisconsin. The one who managed the manufacturing and sales of the furniture. The one who found the suppliers, ordered the materials, paid the bills and collected on the invoices. The one who'd made Schrock Brothers Furniture a business that folks traveled to Miller's Creek for.

The ache was being the last to know when it affected his life. As Gideon sometimes feared, he was just the younger brother who'd tagged along from Ohio and now lathed table legs and dovetailed drawers together. He'd been content with that for some time. And while he did have his own ambitions, they were on his own terms. His stomach churned anew at the prospect of managing people. Bile threatened the back of his throat. He swallowed convulsively. He wasn't sure he wanted to help manage someone else's growing business.

And he wasn't going to stay. Or at least, he hadn't been going to.

But how could he go now when his brother needed him?

If his heart had pounded before at the thought of telling Malachi his plans to leave, it now bolted like a frightened horse whirling about the interior of a small pen. He was trapped. Gideon hooked a thumb under the strap of his suspenders and lifted it away from his chest, hoping the space would allow him to draw in an easier breath.

He knew the warehouse his brother had purchased. He'd heard discussions of the asking price. Malachi had invested serious money. Had perhaps even put his livelihood in jeopardy if the venture failed.

Gideon closed his eyes. He couldn't risk that. Malachi had never let him down. And now he couldn't let Malachi down in this. A series of long breaths finally steadied his racing heart. Jazz, generally antsy to get home, gently nosed his shoulder.

How long would it take for his brother to get this new business established? Could Gideon leave as soon as it was?

Or would he have to continue to put his own dreams on hold? Continuing to live in his brothers' long shadows, wondering if there was anything more to Gideon Schrock than being the older Schrock men's easygoing brother. How long before he lived his own life? Months? Years?

He sighed. All this heavy discussion and he hadn't even gotten an invite to supper. He pressed his hand against his stomach. Probably a good thing as it was rebelling at the prospect of any additions. He led Jazz down the fence to where he'd draped his black coat before playing volleyball and slipped the garment on. He normally didn't get chilly, but the afternoon seemed to have grown a lot colder.

"Don't forget to flip the sign on the window that we're open. It defeats the purpose of having you here if you discourage the customers from coming in."

"That's more your style." Sarah bumped her shoulder against Gideon's bicep. He staggered as if overwhelmed by the onslaught of her slender form but as she stepped back, Sarah narrowed her eyes at his expression. Though he might wear a smile and be ready with a quip, something was bothering him.

"Any more questions before I head out, Sarah?" Malachi asked. "I regret that other than showing you a few things, I haven't left you much time to get settled."

"The cash register is a little different than what I'm used to and the merchandise is much bigger than the goods I've sold before, but I think I'll be okay. I'm sure I'll have many questions by the time you get back."

"Well, if they can't wait until then, just call for Gideon. He'll be in charge here."

Sarah's gaze followed Malachi's tipped head toward Gideon, who looked far from pleased with the pronouncement. What was going on? Was he unhappy she was working here?

Sarah sent a tentative smile in Malachi's direction. "Thank you for this opportunity. I appreciate you hiring me."

"I tried to talk him out of it. Your references are pretty questionable." This time there was a smile in Gideon's eyes to match the one on his lips, but it was a halfhearted one.

Somewhat reassured at his more normal behavior, she snorted softly. "Even though Ben works here, he'd probably have suggested you ask someone else before taking me on. Which makes good sense, because his judgment is questionable as he's chosen you as a close friend."

Gideon's lips barely twitched in acknowledgment of the barb. Her brows furrowed. Was he ill?

"Regardless of what he says, we're glad to have you. And I know you'll do fine." At a series of gentle chimes, Malachi glanced over to a collection of grandfather clocks. "I need to get going. If there is anything Gideon can't handle, I will have a cell phone on me." He grinned. "Bishop approved as there's no phone at the new warehouse yet." With a parting wave, he headed out the door.

Gideon watched him go, frowning, before he turned back to her. "How's the foot?"

She crossed her arms over her chest. "It's finer than you are. Are you all right?"

He furrowed his own brow. "What's that supposed to mean?"

"You just seem...off. And I do mean in the head."

He mirrored her position. "That's a common sentiment coming from you."

Uncrossing her arms, she reached out and touched the tanned skin below his rolled-up sleeve. He almost flinched, hissing in a quiet breath at the action. With a sigh, Sarah pulled her hand back.

"I'm serious, Gideon. Something is wrong. I can see it in you."

He grimaced and turned toward a nearby bedroom suite, taking great interest in the joint of the massive oak dresser. Sarah waited. After a moment, he hunched a muscular shoulder.

"I don't know that I'm manager material."

"You? Lack self-confidence?" Sarah was about to blurt that she couldn't imagine anyone more comfortable in any circumstance, until she realized he was serious. She immediately sobered. "I never realized. Why?"

"I suppose you're right to be surprised. When it's just me, it's not a problem. I can take care of myself. But to be responsible for someone else? Either personal or business-wise? What if I get it wrong?" He turned back to her, his normally affable face solemn.

Sarah's breath caught in her chest. Her heart pounded. She hid a clenched fist, one so tight her short nails dug into her palm, in the folds of her skirt. *I did get it wrong. You're right to worry. It's awful. I'm dealing with the consequences.* The backs of her eyes burned. *So is someone else.*

Gideon tipped his head, his expression shifting at her abrupt reaction. Closing. Sarah drew in a shuddering breath. That was her life and she couldn't change it now. This was about him, and he was obviously hurting. Sarah was surprised at the ache that swept through her at seeing him so. Stretching out her fisted fingers, she again reached out, this time leaving her hand on his arm.

"You can do this."

He smiled faintly. "How do you know? You just started

here. You haven't been here long enough to understand what all 'this' entails."

"I might not know what it entails. But I know you'll do a *gut* job because I know you. You can do this. And very well. Why, I even trust you to be responsible for me."

Gideon's arm moved underneath her fingers. *Was he shifting it to take her hand?* Instead, he reached up to rub the back of his neck. It seemed he was going to rebuff her support. After a brief moment, he subtly bobbed his head and gave her a more genuine Gideon smile.

"Denki."

She returned it. Shoulders she wasn't aware were taut relaxed. "You're welcome. Just don't get a big head."

"No problem there. If I did, the new hat I just got wouldn't fit and I can't afford to buy another one as this 'management job' didn't come with a wage increase."

Gideon searched for a topic that would take attention off him and the alien feelings the touch of her hand and her encouragement had sent surging through him. His new role still seemed daunting and unpalatable, but at least now, he felt like he could tackle it today.

"Any change in Anne's decision?"

With a scowl, Sarah plopped down on a nearby glider, propped her elbows on her knees and rested her cheeks in her palms. *"Nee.* And from as fiercely as she's dug in, I don't know that she'll ever go to school." She morosely shook her head. "How will she get an education?"

"You seem to occasionally have a brain in your head. Could you teach her?"

"Ja. But what with helping my *mamm* with housework and then suppertime, I don't think there's time enough in the evenings when I get off work before Anne goes to bed."

She heaved a sigh. "I suppose I could get her up in the morning before I leave and do some."

Gideon glanced around the currently empty showroom. From the lemony smell of furniture polish, it was obvious she'd already been busy dusting surfaces. "Before you were hired, Malachi was splitting his time between the office, customers and the workshop. A lot of our business is shipped to furniture stores. We are getting more walk-in customers as tourism to the Amish communities grows in town." He grimaced at the reminder. "There's definitely a need for you, but you won't be that busy."

"But I aim to grow that walk-in business even more, so I will be busy." She wrinkled her nose at him.

"All right. But it might take you a week…or maybe even a month, to do so. In the meantime…" He rubbed a hand over his chin as he looked around the showroom. "Would your folks let Anne come in to work with you? She could stay in the office when customers come in. Otherwise you two could work on one of the tables out here. There's not much extra room in the office, but I could put up a whiteboard for you to work with her on. Get her practicing for when she does finally go to school, as I'm sure she eventually will."

His breath caught at the look Sarah gave him. She bounded up from the glider and threw her arms around him. "That's a *wunderbar* idea! *Denki*, Gideon!" His heart bolted when she gave him a quick smooch on the cheek. Instinctively, he lifted his arms to wrap around her, but she stepped back and dropped her own. Thankfully, Sarah didn't notice his response as she started pacing, weaving her way through the nearby rockers and gliders.

"I'd need to get some appropriate books. But I don't think that would be a problem. I can probably get those from Dorothy. And paper and pencils. But I can provide those…"

At her spontaneous embrace, the odd sensations and awareness that he'd clamped down or explained away since their collision yesterday rushed back anew, like a herd of thirsty cattle charging the gate to the water trough in a hot July.

"...could you get it set up?"

"What?" he asked blankly, still dwelling on the slowly receding imprint of her warm form pressed against him.

"The whiteboard. When could you get it set up?"

He reeled his mind in but it was like fighting a ten-pound walleye on the line. "Uh... I think there was some left over from when we put up a section in the shop to keep track of WIP. I'll check to see what's there."

She clasped her hands together. "Great! So when?"

Gideon shook his head as he grinned at her. "If we have it, I'll put it up this afternoon."

The way her eyes lit warmed him considerably. He raised an eyebrow when her face fell.

"Malachi might not approve."

He flexed his jaw. Resentment at being railroaded by his brother into his new, and hopefully short-term, role flared. He was still angry at Malachi. Wasn't proud of it, but there it was. If he was trapped here for a while, he was going to take charge of his cage. "Didn't you hear him? Malachi said I was in charge here. I guess this is my first command decision."

It was one that definitely pleased Sarah. Gideon grimly tamped down the flutters—*flutters!*—her big smile gave him. Now he just needed to get back command of his senses when his long-standing friend was around.

Chapter Four

Sarah slipped the previous day's receipts into the appropriate files. The soft *clunk* when she slid the drawer shut was the only sound in the office and showroom beyond the slow, metronomic ticking of the grandfather clocks. The quietness didn't worry her. She'd peeked around the corner a few minutes ago to check on Anne. Her sister was playing with a doll and cradle in the alcove dedicated to toys that Gideon had established by adding a shoulder-high wall at the back of the store just outside the office.

Ruth Schrock, who'd stopped by with her little ones in a rare moment when Malachi had been present, had gazed at the additions—three walls lined with blocks, farm equipment, trains, doll cradles, marble tracks and child-size tables and chairs—all made of wood by a recent arrival to a nearby district. She'd nudged her husband and asked why he hadn't thought of doing that. Malachi, grinning, had patted Gideon on the back and responded that he didn't need to think of everything when he had a good local manager in place.

Gideon, instead of looking thrilled with the praise, had appeared a little ill. No one else seemed to note how abruptly he'd disappeared through the door to the workshop shortly afterward. Sarah hurt for him, but she didn't know what to do. He may not want to manage, but he was doing a good job of it.

It had been three weeks since he'd invited Sarah to bring Anne to the shop and teach her during lax time. Aiming to not just perform her new job but excel in it, Sarah worked to keep "lax" time to a minimum. After a brief lesson on the systems, much to Malachi's appreciation, she'd taken on the filing and bookkeeping, things she'd done at a previous job. Due to the expansion, Malachi was working on the bishop to allow electronic additions to the business. Sarah itched to learn those as well.

But with as quickly as Anne was gobbling up her schoolwork, even the limited time Sarah had available so far had been ample, leaving space for the girl to quietly play. Sarah twisted her lips. Whatever prompted Anne's resistance, it wasn't at the prospect of learning.

But Sarah knew that already. She leaned on the desk and put her head in her hands.

Anne didn't want to go to school because of her scars.

Her sister was self-conscious because of the hard, thick, red, raised scars that ran down her neck to streak over her chest and back and down her arms. Fortunately, her face had been spared except for a small wedge of red visible on the lower part of one cheek. Sarah shuddered at the thought of more having been affected. The scars made Anne apprehensive around anyone outside the family. For some reason, that wariness had recently amplified. Anne wouldn't say why, even when pressed. But whatever it was, for sure and certain, the scars were at the heart of it.

When Sarah had access to resources, she'd researched all that could be done to minimize the scars. She looked up what she could in the library. She bombarded the doctors with questions at Anne's appointments. Some of the answers had only increased the guilt that continually burdened her.

The time it took for a burn to heal was a strong predictor of scarring. Burns that took more than three weeks to heal, like Anne's, had a higher risk of developing hypertrophic scars. The depth of the burn and how it was initially treated impacted the severity of the scarring and how much its appearance could be reduced. Sarah had learned it could take up to two years for a burn wound to heal. That although the marks wouldn't go away, they would eventually fade over time.

But Anne's weren't fading near fast enough to suit Sarah. Despite the topical creams she rubbed on her sister to help treat the appearance as well as the itching and discomfort, there didn't seem to be much improvement. When Anne would mutely weep after a session, Sarah's pillow would also be wet with tears. If she could have, she'd willingly have taken the scars upon herself, freeing her little sister of them.

The front door of the store chimed. Sarah sprang to her feet, hastily patting her cheeks to add some color. She tucked in loose strands that had worked free from her *kapp* and, pasting on a smile, left the office to greet potential customers.

A tall young man some years older than herself and a middle-aged woman stood just inside the closed front door. Sarah had never seen them before. Their outfits suggested they were from out-of-town. Instead of jeans like most of the locals, they wore dress pants. Their thin, sleek sweaters weren't made of cotton or acrylic, but of fine wool. The woman sported a gold necklace and discreet gold earrings. The young man flashed her an attractive smile.

Her own smile expanded into a more natural one. *Time to sell some furniture.*

"Hello. Anything in particular you're looking for today?"

The woman inhaled deeply. "I just love the smell of furniture shops. The varnish and the wood."

Sarah wove her way toward them through the dining room sets. "Unfortunately, we don't bottle that. But we do have some nice candles made locally by the Amish. I'll ask if they can concoct a 'Furniture Store' scent." Though she inwardly winced at throwing "Amish" into the conversation, she knew "Amish" was what many out-of-town visitors came shopping for.

The woman looked arrested for a moment before bursting into laughter. Its warmness had Sarah chuckling lightly in response.

"I'll have to keep that in mind. In the meantime, I want to check out these beautiful tables and chairs."

"Take your time and let me know if you have any questions. If you don't see what you want, we can make any design in a variety of woods or stains."

The woman nodded with a smile as she trailed her fingers lightly over a counter-height, cherry table. Sarah turned to find the young man watching her, still wearing his attractive smile.

"It's like taking a kid to a candy store. She'll be busy *oohing* and *aahing* and *hmming* for a while."

"Happy to have her do that to her heart's content. While she does, is there anything here that you might be interested in?"

The immediate flare in his eyes and the crinkles appearing at the corners of them told Sarah that what he might be interested in was her. Men had looked at her like that for some years now. It was *hochmut* to admit it and the Amish frowned on pride, but she knew she was pretty. But pretty was as pretty did. And sometimes what pretty did was draw unwanted attention. Thankfully, though the young man's glance was admiring, it was simply that and not creepy. Inviting, in fact.

"Why don't you show me around? What types of furniture do you have? Is it all made here?"

Sarah answered his questions as she proceeded to lead him through the store. He introduced himself as Brad and was easy to talk with, a natural conversationalist. Though Sarah kept an eye on the woman, whom Brad identified as his mother, she was laughing at his wry observations by the time they wandered to the back of the store. She'd forgotten all about Anne until they reached the partial wall separating the children's area from the main showroom.

Brad, looking over the wall, grew suddenly quiet. Sarah stood on tiptoe to peer over to see what had caught his attention. Anne was in the far corner, trying to make herself as small as possible. She was facing away, bent over the doll cradle. With her head tipped forward and her hair up in her miniature *kapp*, the red scars that ran down the back of her neck before disappearing under her collarless dress stood out like bold writing on a page.

Sarah hissed in a breath, ashamed she'd briefly forgotten about her sister. Anne's shoulders immediately hunched up. Still turned away, she slunk along the back wall to disappear around the corner into the office. Sarah bit her lip, mortified for her sister. The backs of her eyes burned. She blinked fiercely. When she'd successfully warded off threatening tears, she found Brad watching her sympathetically.

"Burn?"

"Ja." It was a shaky whisper.

"She must've been very young. Take a while to heal?"

"Ja." Sarah cleared her clogged throat. "How did you know?"

He smiled crookedly. "I went to medical school at the University of Wisconsin and I'm doing my residency at UW Health in Madison. We covered hypertrophic scars. I've seen a few of them at the hospital. The thickness is a result of abnormal or excessive healing." He glanced toward the corner where Anne had disappeared. "They've been getting good results on them with state-of-the-art laser treatments. Does she have any limited mobility due to the scars? Like they won't let an elbow or knee bend as it should?"

"No. The worst scars are mostly down her back and chest. The ones down her arms aren't quite as bad."

Brad nodded thoughtfully. "Laser treatment might also cause softening and less itching. Are you familiar with it?"

Sarah shook her head.

"They can help, though it might not be a dramatic improvement with laser treatment alone. She'd need to be anesthetized." He raised an eyebrow in apparent question if that was an issue. At a single shake of her head, he continued. "But with a comprehensive burn scar reconstructive treatment program tailored for her, including a combination of surgery, tissue expansion or medication, she might see quite an improvement. One that would make a difference in her life."

Sarah steepled her fingers and pressed them against her mouth, trying to restrain her excitement. Anne's disfiguring scars reduced! Her heart rate escalated at the possibility, but... With surgeries and doctors' appointments came costs. How long would she have to work to cover them? Years, if even that would do it. Years that she would need to work. Years delaying marriage. Delaying her own family. Her stomach soured as she momentarily rebelled. But only momentarily. If it would help Anne, that would always be her choice.

She licked her dry lips and swallowed. "I'd like to learn more about this."

"I'd be happy to tell you anything I know and—" he

lifted up his phone "—anything I can research by this or other methods. The residency keeps me pretty busy. Though the shifts are long, I do occasionally get some time off, like this trip with my mom." Brad smiled. "Which now I'm glad I made. I don't suppose you're available for lunch?"

Again, Sarah shook her head, more vigorously this time.

He made a faint moue of disappointment. "Well, there're some other places she'd like to stop in the area that will probably take up the rest of the day. Maybe we could have coffee before we head back to Madison. What time do you get off?"

Gideon froze in the doorway, not sure he'd heard the words correctly with the sounds of the workshop behind him. But it was a pretty sure thing he had, if the blush in Sarah's cheeks as she stared at him over the short wall was anything to go by. Clenching his teeth, his gaze moved to the tall *Englisch* man whose attention had barely shifted from Sarah.

He'd been making it a habit to duck his head into the showroom to "check" on things in the morning and afternoon. See how Anne's studies were doing. Just plain see Sarah. Usually seeing Sarah eased some of the constant tension that pervaded him at knowing he was responsible for the site. Today, it didn't. His tension escalated at seeing her cozily talking with the stranger. Gideon strode into the showroom, glancing into the office as he passed the door. He frowned and slowed at the sight of Anne crouched on the far side of the desk. The little girl shook her head when she met his gaze and put a finger to her lips. Gideon nodded slightly and kept walking.

"Gideon! Is everything all right? Any problems?" Sarah's voice was pitched higher than normal.

"Not back there." As he joined the two, he noticed a middle-aged woman near the front of the store, carefully inspecting the drawers of a large oak hutch. The sight slowed his heart rate a click or two.

"How about here?" He drew in a deep breath, something he'd begun doing around Sarah, trying to catch the faint honeysuckle fragrance. The one that teased him when he should be doing other things. Like working. Or sleeping. But instead of the subtle aroma, a stronger, spicier smell overlaid that of wood and varnish. His brows furrowed. Aftershave? Cologne? It smelled…expensive. He eyed the *Englisch* man before his gaze flicked to Sarah. Would she prefer that over a man's scent of, say, sawdust, hay and horse? He scowled, barely squashing the impulse to herd the man to the front of the store toward his apparent companion.

Unless…unless the young *Englisch* man had come into the store just to visit with Sarah? Uncomfortable with the strange feelings shooting through him, Gideon crossed his arms over his chest and tucked his fisted hands into his armpits. Was this…*jealousy*? Shocked at the possibility, he inhaled sharply, drawing in more of the offensive cologne.

"We're doing fine. Brad and I were just talking about…" Sarah's voice trailed off as she glanced at the office door.

Brad? How often had the young *Englischer* come in? It was good to be friendly to customers. But *Brad*?

"What kind of furniture are you looking for, *Brad*." The smile on Gideon's face didn't match his growl of the man's name.

Brad didn't seem to hear it. He glanced about the showroom. "Not anything in particular. Though I suppose it's time to upgrade from my college furniture." His smile for Sarah was full of perfect white teeth. "I could probably convince Mom to shift a few pieces of furniture to me so she has reason to come here and replace them. I might just tag along again."

"You do that. You're welcome to come in anytime and look for...*furniture.* We also have maps here of other Amish stores in the community. I'm sure Sarah would be happy to get you one." Gideon gave her a pointed look. Anything to put some distance between the two.

Sarah dodged around the furniture to the counter and retrieved a flyer from underneath it. To Gideon's displeasure, the *Englisch* man followed her like a hound on a trail. Gideon pressed his lips together. Unfortunately, shooing potential customers out of the store contradicted his role as manager. But at least now a counter separated Sarah and...*Brad.*

When she frowned askance at him from the counter, Gideon rubbed a hand over his scowl. It wasn't like Sarah couldn't handle herself. He'd watched her over the years do more than a fair job of handling herself with young men from their district and others. He'd just never felt like this while watching before. Whatever the feeling was, he didn't like it.

He headed back to the workshop, bumping a few chairs at his brisk pace. "If you need me, you know where to find me." *I won't chase him out...this time. Sorry about the lost business, Malachi, but I hope I never find that* Englisch *man in here again.* Gideon glanced into the office as he went by and almost swung into it at the sight of Anne's face. She looked as troubled as he felt. At the immediate shake of her head, he grimly proceeded to the workshop. If the door happened to bang when he shut it behind him, *ach,* the wall was solid and could handle a little...feeling.

Chapter Five

The store was, for the moment, quiet. Sarah smiled, slowly inhaling the scent of wood and varnish as she looked over the array of bedroom sets, dining sets, wooden benches, rockers, gliders and Morris mission chairs. Maybe it was possible to come up with such a candle scent. She would indeed ask.

She wandered to the window that looked out into the alley. Gideon, brown bag in one hand and a canned soft drink in another, was exiting the side door of the workshop. Her brother Ben followed, joining him at a shaded picnic table, one made in the shop with scraps of excess wood. A few other men exited as well but continued strolling down the alley, presumably to the Dew Drop restaurant.

She was allowed a lunch break. Interesting—and surprising—as Brad's offer had been earlier that morning, she'd rather have her church spread sandwich at the picnic table with her *bruder* and Gideon than eat lunch with the attractive *Englisch* man. The pair had left shortly after his invitation, but she did hope he came in another time when she could ask more questions about laser treatments for Anne.

When she entered the office to get her lunch, Anne was at the small table they'd set up for her in a corner, carefully printing her ABCs on lined paper. Sarah raised her eyebrows. They'd already done the schoolwork for the day. Her sister was working ahead.

Sarah retrieved their lunch bag and returned to the door. "Come on. We're going to eat lunch out at the picnic table with Ben and Gideon."

Anne didn't look up for her work. "I'm not. I'm eating in here."

Sarah huffed in frustration. Ever since the *Englischers* had been in this morning, Anne had refused to leave the office. Had barely even acknowledged Sarah when she'd checked on her earlier. "Are you sure? It's nice outside. Probably one of the last nice days we're going to have before it turns cold."

Anne got a fresh piece of paper and began printing numbers. "I'm sure."

Sighing, Sarah fished Anne's sandwich and the plastic baggie of homemade potato chips out of the bag and set them on the corner of the desk. With a "make sure you eat" admonishment, she retraced her steps to the front of the store to flip the Out to Lunch sign before slipping out the door and descending the sidewalk steps to head down the alley. When she slid onto the wooden seat next to Ben, she was greeted with a nod from him and a surprising scowl from the table's other occupant.

She pulled her sandwich out of the bag and raised an eyebrow at him. "What's the matter with you?"

Gideon's response was a grunt. "Sell anything to the *Englischers*?"

"Not yet. But I think I will." She grinned as she met his gaze.

"Not surprised. They looked like they were interested in…something." He lifted his own sandwich to his mouth.

Sarah eyed Gideon's sandwich with its substantial portion of meat between two thick slices of homemade bread. With Ben now married and not living at home, Gideon hadn't been in her *mamm*'s kitchen for a long time. She tore off a chunk of bread crust smeared with the peanut butter and marshmallow crème church spread combination and popped it into her mouth.

"That looks like meatloaf." She nodded at his sandwich. "When did you learn to cook?"

Ben grinned. "He didn't. He doesn't have to. You'd be surprised at all the food that gets dropped off at his place."

"The way to a man's heart... Or so they say." Gideon mumbled around another bite.

Sarah looked at her thin sandwich and set it down on its wrapper. She'd lost her appetite. "Who brought that over? Someone who's well on her way to your heart?"

The tanned column of Gideon's throat bobbed as he swallowed. His grumpy expression cleared as he squinted at the opposite building. "I don't recall. I don't think it's the same one who brought the apple pie that's currently sitting on my counter. Or the peach one that's in the refrigerator. I think they've found the way to my stomach, but are still missing the map to my heart. I'll have to let them keep trying." He dropped his gaze to her. "When are you going to fix me something?"

Sarah scowled and gave him a half-hearted kick under the table.

Gideon winced. "Ow. Your foot must be completely healed."

"Enjoy it. That's about all you'll get from me."

He made a production out of examining his sandwich before frowning thoughtfully. "Maybe that's all I want."

Suppressing a smile, she swung her foot to kick him

harder. Gideon dodged it, shifting farther down the bench where he took another bite of his sandwich.

Ben shook his head. "My twins are more mature than you two and they're not long out of diapers."

Sarah opened her mouth to retort when a flash of color at the street drew her attention as a car parked in front of the store. Four *Englisch* women got out. One of them shaded a hand over her eyes as she looked toward the store's front entrance before turning to the others and they began a discussion.

Sarah jumped up, stuffed her uneaten sandwich back into its paper bag and shoved it toward her brother. "I need to go."

Gideon's brows furrowed. "You're allowed a break. You've barely had one. You can stay a bit longer."

She slid out from the picnic table. "Chance for a sale. Maybe I can move some of your shoddy work." Throwing him a smile, she brushed her hands down the front of her skirt and headed up the alley toward the car, the quickest way to reach the quartet before they left.

Gideon watched Sarah go, her skirt swinging with her determined stride.

Ben followed his gaze. "She likes the job. It's more of a challenge than her last one."

"She's doing well at it." Gideon wadded up his own wrapper and stuck it in his bag. Opening his soda, he focused on the pop tab to keep his gaze from again following Sarah. Ben might be on the quiet side, but his friend didn't miss much. Gideon raised the can and took a long drink. The meatloaf had been a little dry. Or maybe it was because as soon as Sarah sat down, the scent of honeysuckle had wafted to him. He'd drawn it in, faint but steady, with each inhalation. Any interest in his sandwich had deserted him. The cold meatloaf wasn't any competition for the honeysuckle.

Figuring it was safe to finally do so, he oh-so-casually looked toward the street to see her chatting with the *Englischers*. A moment later, Sarah and the four women disappeared from view in front of the building.

Gideon finished the soda and crinkled the can in his hand. Malachi was at the warehouse, as he had been every day, only stopping in here to go over any needed paperwork after everyone else had left the workshop. His brother had hired a few local Amish boys—those too old to be in school and not busy working with their families during harvest—to help him clean out the warehouse. Gideon had offered his assistance, even after hours—anything to get the warehouse up and running as soon as possible—but Malachi had declined, telling him he was more valuable at the shop. Then he'd shown Gideon his system of inventory and reorder points for the various materials needed to build the furniture, along with his list of suppliers, and patted him on the back.

A pat that had felt like one of the large solid oak china cabinets had fallen on him. A pat that could suffocate him with very little effort.

Some aspects of this supervisory thing weren't bad. He actually enjoyed managing the supply chain. Malachi reassured him he was doing a good job. Fellow employees had no problem with him in charge. He seemed to be the only one who did. He didn't want the responsibility. What if he ran them out of a critical piece of inventory? Got someone hurt? Messed up and lost a big customer that Malachi had worked hard to get?

Gideon inhaled sharply, drawing Ben's attention.

"Have you ever felt like leaving?" It burst from him in response to Ben's raised eyebrow.

"Leaving what?" Ben raised the other one. "The job?"

"The job. The town." Now that the question was out there, Gideon caught himself holding his breath at his friend's response. He concentrated on easing the tension from his shoulders as he slowly exhaled.

"Not since I saw Rachel." Ben's eyes softened at the mention of his wife. He smiled crookedly. "And definitely not since Aaron left her and it looked like I had some hope in that direction." His gaze narrowed on Gideon. "Why? You thinking about leaving?"

"No." Gideon quickly schooled his avid interest into nonchalance. "Just...thinking."

Ben nodded as he opened his own drink. "If Rachel had married Aaron, I might have. There didn't seem to be much for me here at that time. At least to my mind. Then Aaron left. Though that definitely changed things for Rachel and me, it also made me realize how much I...love my family."

He blushed, as if the admission was embarrassing. Gideon understood. He loved his brothers, but admitting that to someone else? *Ach*, he'd probably blush too.

Ben cleared his throat. "But now that I'm with Rachel and since Aaron's back—" he nodded at Gideon "—and married to your sister, the family seems complete again. I can't imagine leaving. I have to admit, I look forward to the future gatherings. Seeing my *kinner* go racing off with Aaron's when we get together. And with Sarah's, whenever and whoever she might finally settle down with. Along with my younger siblings' children too when they reach that age." He smiled self-consciously. "I sound like my *mamm*. I can't imagine what it would do to her if one of us left again. It about tore her up when Aaron left. But having had one gone for a while makes me realize how...precious and important it is to have everyone together."

"*Ja*. Family is important." Gideon worked as hard to manufacture a smile to share with his friend as he had assembling the tambour for a roll-top desk earlier this morning. He'd loved his folks, but he'd learned to live without them in the years since he'd left them and his younger siblings to move with Malachi, Samuel and later Miriam, to Wisconsin. He couldn't imagine being here without those three. Ben's vision brought up a tantalizing view of the same situation with the four Schrocks in Miller's Creek. With his little tow-headed children trailing after their cousins at various gatherings throughout the year.

He pushed to his feet. But that dream came at the cost of another. Of experiencing another part of the country. Of maybe a small, single proprietorship business where he was responsible for only himself without worrying about letting anyone else down. Of stepping out of the furrow plowed by his brothers and making his own path.

Which was more important?

For sure and certain, he'd learned one thing though. Ben's words made him remember that when he left, it would be at a cost. When he went, he'd be going alone. Whatever these strange...feelings he was having regarding Sarah, he couldn't pull her away from her family.

Gideon glanced back at the *creak* sounding behind him, checking that the jolt over the pothole hadn't shifted his wagon load. To his relief, the stacks of walnut and maple boards that he'd picked up from the rural Amish lumber mill were still stable.

"Come on, boys," he mildly chastised the Belgian geldings. "You see those potholes before I do. You're supposed to work your way around them." The two draft horses ignored him to continue their steady *clip-clop* down the blacktopped country road.

Gideon leaned back to take in the canopy of bronze leaves above him. He brushed one from the brim of his hat as others drifted down to scatter over him and the boards. Though anyone could have made the trip, he was glad he'd done it himself. Ben was perfectly capable of supervising the workshop for a while. Managing involved delegating, didn't it? And on such a pretty fall day, it was good to get out of the building.

He scowled as he absently brushed a few more leaves off the wooden seat beside him. It was good to have gotten away for other reasons as well. It would've been too difficult to have stayed out of the office. He would've found some reason to work in there as he wanted to comfort—Gideon jerked upright at the word. Goliath, one of the geldings, swiveled an ear back to see if there was something he and Hercules should be concerned about. Gideon lightly tapped the reins on the Belgian's broad back to apologize.

Comfort? Where had that word come from? It was just being a *gut* friend to be concerned when Sarah seemed fretful and distracted this morning when he'd checked in to, *ach*, just check in as he did every morning. When a quick glance around didn't reveal her younger sister, for a moment, he really was concerned. Anne was frail enough as it was. Was she ill? She'd acted a bit strange when he saw her in the office yesterday. Of course, he'd acted strangely as well when he'd seen her sister talking so cozily with the *Englischer*.

Before he could ask, Sarah had blurted that Anne had gone to school, actual school, for the first time that morning.

"I thought this was what you were working toward? You don't seem happy about it."

"*Ja,* but... What if she gets upset? What if whatever was bothering her from going continues to bother her? What if she needs me?"

Gideon wasn't sure if he answered correctly, but his response must've been all right, as Sarah had thrown him an appreciative smile before turning to the customers who'd come through the door with a jingle of the overhead bell. When he'd poked his head in later to advise he was leaving to pick up the lumber, she'd said she was fine, an assertion belied by the strain on her face. With customers still in the store, it wasn't the time to discuss. But Gideon intended to pursue the topic, and maybe one regarding the *Englischer* from yesterday, when he returned.

At a flash of movement, his gaze whipped toward the passing woods. There it was again. Something, or someone, had ducked behind one of the large oak trees that stretched tall just beyond the barbed wire fence. "Ho, boys!" Harnesses jangled as the horses drew to a halt. Gideon shifted to face the oak trees where their leaves now spread over the ground in a golden brown carpet. With the reins woven loosely through his fingers, he propped his elbows on his thighs and peered into the timber.

"I think there's a big rabbit hiding in the woods." Gideon pitched his voice so any listening rabbit—or two-legged creature—lurking among the oaks' broad trunks could hear. "If not a rabbit, maybe it's a squirrel."

The white splash of a *kapp* against the rust and brown background revealed the hider's position as she peeked around a tree.

"Definitely a squirrel. *Guder daag,* Anne. This would certainly be my choice of a place to spend the day."

Gideon casually scratched his cheek as more of the girl emerged from behind the rough-barked trunk. "I'm a little curious, though. Your sister said you'd gone to school this morning. Are you learning your ABCs today from the acorns, the bullfrogs and the caterpillars?"

Anne folded her thin arms across her chest. "I left."

Gideon made a production out of looking about the thick stands of trees on both sides of the road. "As there's no schoolhouse nearby, I guess I can see that." Gentling his voice, he continued. "And although I can't see them, I would imagine there are those who are pretty worried about where you might be right now."

Anne's slender arms tightened further about herself. "There are some who aren't." Her lips pressed into a line straighter than the barbed wire fence that stretched between them.

Gideon secured the reins and stepped down from the wagon. "Are those people important to you?" He crossed the shallow ditch and stopped on his side of the fence.

"Nee!" Anne declared, but her little mouth trembled as she slowly crunched through the leaves to face him.

Reaching over the fence, Gideon tucked his hands under her arms and easily lifted her light weight above the wire to set her down beside him. "If they aren't important to you and you're doing what you know to be right, what difference does it make what they think?"

"Because they make other people look at me." A tear, one unseemly large for her small face, leaked down her cheek. "And laugh."

His heart clenched for her. Out of his depth—he wasn't sure he could truly figure out big girls, much less little ones—Gideon sank down to sit in the ragged grass in front of the fence. "That's rough. I think I'd want to go live in the woods too."

Anne settled cross-legged beside him and sighed heavily.

Her slight weight tipped against his side. The late morning light that filtered through the trees highlighted her red scars, ones visible above the edge of her collarless dress and beyond the ends of her sleeves, making them look like a bold embroidered pattern on her otherwise smooth, white skin.

They sat quietly for a few moments, the only sounds the drone of a few flies and the occasional stomp of the patiently waiting Belgians' shod, bucket-sized hooves.

Gideon plucked a few of the tall grass stems. "I'm playing hooky myself. I don't want to be at work."

"Why not? Everyone is so nice there. Even my sister."

"I have to do things I don't want to. I'd rather hide in the woods and not have to worry about responsibilities."

"I thought you were in charge. Who's making you do things?"

"My brother Malachi," Gideon responded glumly. He sighed. "But he's not making me do them. I'm doing them for him, because I love and respect him. And I don't want to let him down." He rubbed a hand over the back of his neck. "I don't want to disappoint him." He smiled lopsidedly at Anne. "Maybe similar to the way you feel about Sarah."

Anne's head bobbed in a slow nod.

"It's difficult when you love someone and what they think is best for you isn't what you think is best for you." Gideon freed an acorn from where it was tangled in the grass and tossed it onto the road. It skittered across the black asphalt surface. "Maybe they're wrong." He found and pitched another one. They both watched as it rolled behind one of the Belgians' huge hooves and was smashed when the horse took a step back. "But maybe they're right because they know us pretty well and care about us."

"Sarah's embarrassed about me. She wants me to have more surgeries." The words were no more than a whisper.

Gideon frowned. Anne hadn't been much more than a toddler when he'd moved to Miller's Creek, but she'd already had the scars. During the many times he'd been at the Raber household, it was never said how she got them. Sarah always seemed to be the one who took charge of her younger sister's care, before and after the many treatments Anne had had over the years. Before Ben married, Gideon had been at the Raber house late one evening after Anne had gone to bed. The little girl had woken up crying. It was Sarah whom she called for and Sarah who'd raced upstairs to comfort her. It could be that, as was common with the oldest daughter, Sarah had taken on a lot of care for her younger siblings. But the bond between the two seemed more than that.

One thing he knew, Sarah would do anything for Anne.

"Is that why you didn't want to go to the shop with her today?"

Another heavy nod.

"Sarah cares for you deeply. I don't think she's embarrassed about you."

When Anne didn't respond, he scooched farther down the ditch and braced himself on his elbows so his head was level with hers. "Where did you hear about more surgeries?"

"The *Englisch* man was talking to her about them yesterday."

"If he was talking English, how did you understand?"

Anne rolled her eyes at him. "I've been to doctors enough to understand the *Englischer* words for scars and surgery. He's some kind of medical person."

Hmm. Gideon took a moment to absorb that bit of information. He gently touched a raised red line that peeked from below the sleeve of her blue dress. "Does it hurt?"

"*Nee.* Not that one. But sometimes it itches."

"Do you want more surgeries?"

Anne shook her head.

"Even on the ones that hurt and itch?"

She shook her head again as she touched the scar behind her neck. "I'm tired of surgeries. I've had these as long as I can remember, so I guess I can live with always having them. I just don't want Sarah to be embarrassed of me."

"Oh, little one. I think she just wants to help you. I sincerely think that if she could, Sarah would take the scars on herself, just so you didn't have to live with them."

Anne tipped her head as she considered his words but didn't say anything. They sat quietly for a moment as the blue jays called in the timber above them. Gideon dug another acorn out of the grass. Instead of tossing it, he rolled the little capped nut between his fingers.

"You're pretty smart to have learned some English already. You know you'll learn even more if you go back to school. I suppose I need to go back and face my responsibilities too. Although it has been unseasonably warm for Wisconsin this late in the year, it's going to turn cold. Even if the cold doesn't get me, I think I'd get hungry soon. The berries are already pretty well gone for the year. I could only live so long on walnuts and these little acorns. And I'd have to fight the squirrels for them." Anne giggled when Gideon bumped her with his elbow.

"We're Amish. We're not supposed to fight," she admonished with a grin.

He flicked the top off the cap of the acorn and examined it. "Doesn't mean the thought doesn't cross my mind sometimes."

Anne's smile transformed into a firm line and her eyes narrowed. "I know."

Gideon flicked the nut away, put his hands behind his head and leaned back. "Who calls attention to you?"

She scowled. From the way her mouth tightened even further, Gideon wasn't sure he would get an answer.

"Timothy Hochstetler." The name came grudgingly.

Gideon watched fluttering leaves that clung stubbornly to the oak branches stretching overhead. The Hochstetlers were a family of all boys. Thirteen of them if he recalled right, with the oldest around his age. He knitted his brows as he tried to place where a Timothy might fit in the horde of younger Hochstetlers. Other than his nieces and nephews and a few scattered others including Ben's children, he didn't usually keep track of the district's *kinner* below age twelve. But if he remembered correctly, Timothy was the last of the Hochstetler pack.

His mouth tipped down as he recalled his earlier years with his older brothers. Amish might not believe in violence or fighting, but brothers didn't always get along like it was Sunday morning at church. Sometimes they harassed and picked on one another. Frequently it rolled downhill by age. His lips twitched. *Ach*, his brothers still teased him and he was as big, if not bigger, than they were. But that didn't make it right for young Timothy to pick on someone else.

"Friends would help when someone troubles you. There's safety in numbers."

"I don't know how to make them. I'm not pretty and popular like Sarah."

Gideon tilted his head to look at her. "I think you're pretty." He was just about to add "pretty silly," but the look in her eyes advised it wasn't a time for teasing.

"Do you really?"

He straightened up to rest on his elbows again. "I really do." His voice was as solemn as hers. It was true. Anne had the delicate features and blue eyes that made her sister so beautiful.

"When I get older, do you think someone would want to marry me, even with the scars?"

"When you meet the right man, Anne. I think he'd be honored to marry you, and a fool not to, even with the scars."

She nodded thoughtfully. Gideon hissed out a quiet breath. How did he get into such a deep—and important—conversation, lying in the ditch with stiff grass stems poking into his back? At least the conversation seemed to have passed a critical hump. Anne was now smiling faintly. She cocked her head to squint at him. Gideon immediately mistrusted the impish look that glinted there.

"Are you going to marry my sister?"

Chapter Six

Gideon jackknifed into a sitting position. That still didn't seem enough distance between him and Anne's question. Perhaps because it was one that had been nibbling at him in unguarded moments? A ridiculous question with an obvious answer. He lurched to his feet and slid his suddenly damp palms down the front of his pants.

"*Nee.* Your sister and I are just friends."

Anne pushed to her feet as well and brushed off the back of her skirt. "You seem like the right man for her," she persisted.

"We're *good* friends. That's all." He lunged out of the ditch fast enough the Belgians threw their massive heads up in alarm. Gideon immediately slowed his approach to the wagon. "Whoa, boys. It's all right," he soothed them. He turned to find Anne at his elbow, frowning in obvious disappointment.

"I guess that makes you a fool, then."

"You're probably right." He hoisted her into the wagon and climbed up beside her. *Little one, the foolish thing would be to fall for your sister. Knowing I can't have her because she'd want to stay here with her family. Knowing that if I did fall, leaving her would break my heart. And I'm not foolish enough to do that.*

He gathered up the reins. The command to put the geldings in motion was on the tip of his tongue when he paused.

"Hold out your hands," he instructed his passenger.

Glancing at him from under lowered brows, Anne did so, the scars on her wrist and above more visible with her hands extended.

"You ever drive a team before?"

"*Nee*. No one ever lets me do much around the horses." Her scowl informed him it was a decision she disagreed with.

Gideon carefully maneuvered her small fingers around the supple leather. "You can drive back to school."

"Really!" Anne's face lit up.

Probably the most excited the girl had ever been about her education. "I said so, didn't I?" Having advised her of the commands to call to the draft horses, and adding his own voice when the geldings just twitched their ears at the unfamiliar childish one, Gideon laced his fingers together at the back of his head under his hat and leaned back, and for the first time, enjoyed supervising.

They approached the white, one-room schoolhouse just as children were streaming out the door. Some raced for the two outhouses, while others fanned out to take up positions on the grassy ball field with its makeshift backstop.

"Looks like you're just in time for recess."

From the way her shoulders tightened at his comment, recess didn't have the appeal for his small companion that it had had for him. She relaxed again as he coached her through turning the team into the schoolyard.

"That a girl." Gideon gave Anne a grin and a nod as she competently drew the team to a halt and set the brake, earning a small smile in return.

His gaze narrowed as a car slowed on the road beyond

the ball field. Gideon watched it pull to a stop straddling the blacktop and the grassy shoulder. *Englischers*, a man and two women, got out and walked to the fence that bordered the ball field just beyond the lane. Another car pulled up behind it to do the same, adding two more women to the fence.

Though it was obvious the *kinner* were aware of their presence, the children ignored the newcomers until a ball was hit deep into right field, rolling within a few yards of the fence. The young girl playing that position dashed after it. She slowed to a trot, then a hesitant walk as she got closer to the ball, the fence and the watching *Englischers*.

On the crisp fall day, the dialogue was audible up the short lane.

"Oh, isn't she cute with her little dress and bonnet!"

"That's not a bonnet. It's called a *kapp*. They have to wear them all the time. They don't cut their hair either."

One of the women patted her own short hair. "Oh my, I wonder how long their hair gets? To their hips? Their knees?"

The right fielder snatched the ball from the grass. She backed up a few steps before turning and racing with it to the infield where the other children were now all watching.

Gideon jumped down from the wagon and reached up to lift Anne down. When she shook her head, he retreated a step to let her scramble awkwardly down on her own.

From the schoolhouse's shallow steps, the young blond teacher headed in their direction, her eyes wide in question. When they landed on the slight figure beside him, her shoulders slumped in obvious relief.

"Anne! Where had you gone? I was so worried."

The girl beside him stiffened. "No worries," Gideon interceded. He searched his memory for the teacher's name.

Dorcas? Dora? No, it was something longer. What was the matter with him? He never forgot a pretty woman's name. And this one was definitely pretty. Dorothy! That was it.

"The fault was mine, Dorothy. I'd mentioned when Anne was at the shop yesterday that I was picking up lumber today and we…came to a bit of an agreement."

Anne twisted her head to stare at him, her eyes wide. He gave her a wink. He might have mentioned in her hearing that he was picking up lumber today. They *had* come to a sort of agreement. If the two were not quite related, well, the schoolteacher would survive without the knowledge. To his delight, Anne gave him a careful wink back.

"Well, please don't do it again. I was very worried about you." She smiled at Anne. The one she offered Gideon was even wider. "Sarah would never forgive me if something happened to you."

Gideon dipped his chin in acknowledgment as he scanned the *kinner* seated behind a wing of the backstop, awaiting their turn at bat. Catching the eye of a young girl maybe slightly older than Anne, he motioned to her. The *maedel* jumped to her feet and dashed over to skid to a halt before him.

"*Oncle* Gideon! What are you doing here?"

He tugged gently on one of the ribbons of her *kapp*. "I stopped by to make sure you were staying in line, Lily. You're not giving your new teacher any trouble, are you?"

"Oh, *nee*." The girl shook her head vigorously, almost dislodging the smudged *kapp* perched on her blond hair. "I wouldn't do that to Miss Wagler."

Gideon cocked his eyebrow in mock disbelief before shifting so Anne, who stood with her arms crossed over her narrow chest and her head tucked down into hunched shoulders—looking much like a tentative turtle—was in view. He placed a light hand on her frail shoulder, counting it as a victory when she didn't flinch away.

"I've discovered another superb horsewoman." He squatted down to Anne's level. "Do you know my niece?"

Anne made a barely discernible movement with her head. Gideon didn't know if it was a nod or a shake. He wouldn't have heard the "I've seen her," that followed from her motionless lips if he hadn't been crouched right beside her.

"Lily is my older *bruder* Samuel's daughter. He's the local horse trader. I think Lily could give him a run for his money regarding what there is to know about horses. Lily, why don't you tell Anne about the horses you and Samuel are currently working with? Have you gotten any new ones from the track lately?"

Lily eyed him with her own cocked brow before looking back at Anne with a smile and another energetic nod. "Oh, *ja!* We just got in a pretty bay filly. She's the sweetest goer."

"How old?" The question was barely more than a breath, but Anne's eyes sparked with excitement.

"She'll soon turn four. I asked my *daed* if I could have her for my own, but he just grinned and said that would make Patches sad."

"Who's Patches?"

Gideon stood and dropped his hand when Anne's question was accompanied by a step toward Lily.

"He's my pony. And I suppose he might get a little sad if I had another horse. I told *Daed* that Patches could become my younger brothers' pony and I could have the filly. But he said the boys aren't big enough for a pony yet." She propped a hand on her narrow hip. "I suppose he's right, as Micah can't even walk yet. But she is so pretty. And so fast."

"What's her name?" No longer hunched up, Anne took

another step toward Lily. With her stick-thin arms, she looked pale and slight next to his sun-browned and robust niece.

"She has a long track name, but I just call her Fancy. *Daed* says that's okay. He's starting to call her that too."

"How many horses do you have?"

Before Anne's question could be answered, Lily's name was hollered from the direction of the ball field. "It's your turn at bat!"

Lily waved a hand in response and called, "Go ahead without me." She turned back to Anne. "Let's go sit on the swing and I'll tell you about them all." Lily reached out and grabbed the other girl's hand. Anne hesitated for a brief moment before allowing herself to be tugged along.

Gideon exhaled in relief as he watched the two skipping toward a primitive swing set. When he glanced over to the schoolteacher, she was all but wringing her hands together as she looked over her shoulder toward right field. Gideon followed her gaze. The *Englischers* were leaning on the fence like they'd settled in for the duration.

Another child was at bat, but the way the young pitcher—along with the rest of the children—kept looking back at their unexpected audience, the boy would never find the strike zone. Gideon frowned. When Dorothy's gaze returned to him, her brows knit with concern, he nodded and summoned a reassuring smile. She responded with such a look of gratitude his eyebrows rose.

"I've got to get into town with this lumber," Gideon tipped his head toward the loaded wagon. "They're probably wondering if I took a wrong turn or something. I'll take care of that on my way by." He climbed up onto the driver's seat. As he gathered the reins, he glanced in the direction of the swing set. Lily gave him an enthusiastic wave, Anne's was considerably more subdued, but was still a wave. He returned the farewell, guided the team in a semicircle to exit the small schoolyard and pulled out onto the road.

The parked cars didn't leave him a lot of room to get by, but as he anticipated, the quintet at the fence drifted toward the road as he approached with the team and wagon. He drew the geldings to a halt.

"You folks doing all right? You need some directions?"

"We just stopped to watch the children play. They look so adorable in their dresses and bonnets." The female speaker glanced at one of the other women, winced and continued. "I mean *kapps*."

Gideon smiled. "If you're headed for Miller's Creek, there are some fine shops in town. I can recommend the furniture store, if you'd like to look around. And if you want to stop in at the Dew Drop restaurant, they make a fine lunch. Both places have maps available of the Amish businesses in the countryside, as several have opened in the last few years."

"That sounds like a good idea." One of the women stepped close to pat the nearest Belgian on his nose. Gideon was glad it was one of the tranquil draft geldings and not his high-strung Standardbred mare who would have reacted much differently to the unexpected attention. He just hoped the immense horse didn't shift one of his huge, shod hooves and accidentally step on the woman.

"Speaking of the furniture store, I need to get this—" he hooked a thumb toward the stacked lumber behind him "—delivered there." He made a show of eyeing the road ahead and rubbed a hand across his chin. "It might be helpful if you could pull on down the road and give me a little more room for these big boys. Goliath is an old hand at traffic, but Hercules here is getting adjusted and is a little more skittish." Gideon hoped the ten-year-old horse, a pro with traffic and capable of pulling a load through a space so narrow you had to grease the walls to get through, would forgive him for the slight.

"Oh, certainly! Of course!" With a flurry of agreements the *Englischers* obligingly headed to their cars. They rolled down the windows and waved as they carefully pulled away.

Gideon waved back and called after them. "And if they have any left at the restaurant, try the sweet rolls. They're *wunderbar*!"

He watched over his shoulder as the cars drove past the schoolhouse, albeit slowly, and continued down the road. He didn't have a problem with most *Englischers*. Some he even regarded as *gut* friends. He just felt…uncomfortable having his life and his community considered as something of a spectator activity. Something he wouldn't tell his *bruder,* as *Englischers* made up a significant part of Schrock Brothers Furniture business. That was all well and good, but as for himself, he'd prefer a job that was more focused on goods for his community.

With a sigh, he sought out the schoolteacher. Apparently watching for him, she gave a big wave. Even from this distance he could see her smile. After one last check of the two at the swing set, whose heads were now so close together they might have been a double-yolked egg, he instructed the geldings to "walk on."

Gideon squinted at the sun as they headed down the now empty road. He was going to be much later getting back to the shop than he'd figured. *Ach*, his goal had been to get away from it for a while. That was why he, as *supervisor*, had assigned himself to the task. He grimaced. They'd do fine without him anyway. He may be a Schrock of Schrock

Brothers, but Ben was actually more suited to a supervisory role. Too bad they couldn't adopt him into the family.

His lips twitched. He'd be glad to have Ben as a true brother. He could see himself as a sibling to Anne as well. They almost were, with Aaron Raber married to his sister Miriam. Might as well adopt the whole family.

But if Aaron, Ben and Anne were his siblings, that would mean Sarah was as well. The thought gave a curious—and unpleasant—twist to his stomach. He didn't want Sarah as a sister. He scrubbed a hand down his face. He wanted her as…as a *gut* friend, just like he'd told Anne. He had sisters, but he didn't have many *gut* female friends.

He gave one last look over his shoulder at the schoolhouse that was diminishing in the distance and relaxed back on the seat. He might be late getting back to work, but it had still been a productive morning.

When the shop door chimed, Sarah grimaced faintly. *Why didn't I put the Closed sign up when I was out there a bit ago?* Normally thrilled with a customer no matter how late, today she just wanted to go home and see how Anne's first day of school had gone. After quickly but meticulously jotting down the receipt she was recording, she pushed to her feet and left the office. Rounding the corner, she stopped in surprise to see Dorothy running her fingers over one of the glass-smooth tabletops.

"Well, hello! I didn't expect to see you here. But I'm glad you are. I was just thinking about school."

"It was a *wunderbar* day today."

"Really?" Sarah arched her eyebrows in surprise at the effusive response. *Maybe Anne had a good day after all?* She opened her mouth to ask.

"Did—"

"Is Gideon here?" Her friend was blushing. And had a sparkle in her eyes. All while asking about Gideon.

Sarah's response was decidedly lacking in enthusiasm. "Malachi called earlier this afternoon and wanted Gideon to come over to the new warehouse about something. He hasn't returned yet. I don't know when, or if, he will today."

"Oh." The smile stayed but the sparkle definitely faded. "I just wanted to thank him."

Sarah crossed her arms over her chest. "I'm sure he'll appreciate that. About what?"

"He rescued me today."

Another blush. Sarah almost rolled her eyes but instead cocked her head in question.

"Anne ran away during first recess."

"What!" Sarah's arms flung wide. Her heart began to gallop. "Oh no! Is she all right? Is she back?" She was almost to the door before Dorothy caught up to her and touched her arm.

"I'm so sorry. I shouldn't have said it like that. She's fine." Dorothy smiled. "She's more than fine. When Gideon brought her back, he called Lily over and helped the two girls make a connection over horses. Lily took Anne under her wing and the two became inseparable for the rest of the afternoon. Lily even walked part of the way with Anne when your siblings headed home this afternoon." Her brows knit. "Were your families in separate districts earlier? I'm surprised the girls weren't more familiar with each other through church and other community functions."

Sarah hunched a shoulder. She didn't want to admit that she'd supported, maybe even encouraged, Anne's isolation whenever her sister had expressed any sort of discomfort or hesitation about being with other children. Anything to protect her. Anne had been through so much with the surgeries at such a young age.

Sarah sank onto a nearby ottoman with knee-weakening relief that Anne was safe. "You're sure she was all right? Where did she go? Where did Gideon find her?"

Dorothy shook her head. "I don't know about that. But for sure and certain, she was all right. I think I even saw a smile."

Sarah's eyebrows lifted. Anne usually only smiled around her.

"And as she left, she said she'd see me tomorrow. So all's well that ended well. Thanks to Gideon." Dorothy glanced toward the workshop's closed door. A little too wistfully, in Sarah's opinion. "When you see him, would you please thank him for me?"

"*Ja.* For certain." *After I grill him about what happened.* She rose and flipped the sign to Closed as the schoolteacher opened the door.

Dorothy paused before stepping outside. "I'm so glad to have someone I already count as a *gut* friend."

Sarah's returning smile flickered with guilt. She'd been hoping for one herself as all her buddy bunch had married off. But had she been that *gut* a friend? How could she blame Dorothy for chasing Gideon when most all of the single women in the district already had? It wasn't as if she had a claim on him herself. She reached out to gently squeeze Dorothy's hand. "Me too. So glad you moved into the area."

She watched as her friend climbed into her buggy. Maybe she'd told Dorothy wrong. Maybe Gideon was back and just hadn't stopped up front like he usually did. Sarah crossed to the workshop door and looked out to see the men cleaning up their workstations for the day. They glanced up and nodded in her direction. At her question if there'd been any sign of Gideon, there was a collective shake of heads. She quietly closed the door.

Gideon had smiled as he'd stepped into the office with the paperwork from the lumber mill when he'd returned this afternoon. But that wasn't strange. A smile, whether one of ready amusement or inner perspective on life's absurdities, was something he wore almost as frequently as his flat-brimmed straw hat. Although she *had* caught him a few times lately watching her with a more serious expression on his face. Sarah frowned. She'd have to ask him about that. Malachi's call today had come in before they could speak. With a parting wave, Gideon had left immediately after.

Now, with Dorothy's news, she wanted to ask Gideon about finding Anne. She'd been shocked at her sister's adamant determination to go to school today instead of coming into the shop with her. Shocked and a little hurt when Anne wouldn't say why. Had Anne shared with Gideon why she'd abruptly changed her mind about school? About why she'd left it so soon the first day? How had he convinced her to return? Sarah would offer her thanks along with Dorothy's. Thank him herself for apparently being so convincing that Anne stayed. Thank him for introducing her sister to a friend.

Sarah smiled as her fingers stroked over a roll-top desk she knew was largely Gideon's work. Speaking of friends, he was a very true one. From what Malachi had let slip, she'd been a candidate for the job due to Gideon. They'd had many good times when he'd come over to visit when Ben still lived at home. Gideon had made it fun when they'd been paired together by brides at weddings, occasions that could have been awkward with the pointed glances thrown their way, implying they were a couple.

Even though a short while ago she'd been eager to get home, Sarah lingered in the store, straightening things that didn't need straightening, dusting surfaces that didn't need dusting, while she listened to the ticking of the grandfather clock and waited for Gideon to return. The surfaces were all glass-smooth and every knickknack and pillow was neatly organized when she finally peeked into the workroom door. The workshop, with only skylights for illumination, was empty and growing dark. Gideon obviously wasn't coming back here tonight.

With a sigh, Sarah closed up the front of the store and harnessed her horse. As it was Friday night and not a Church Sunday, she wouldn't see him again until Monday. The start of the workweek seemed like a long time away. Too long. Especially when she felt a bit...unsettled.

Anne liked Gideon. No surprise there, as every female between the ages of one and one hundred seemed to, but Sarah had observed her sister around Gideon. Anne trusted him, really trusted him. As in, might tell him things Anne wasn't sharing with her.

Sarah ran a hand down Toffee's neck before climbing into the buggy, trying to soothe the sting that, for the first time, Anne hadn't shared everything with her. Hadn't shared, when Sarah had always taken care of her. Had always been there for her. Even before... Sarah squeezed her eyes shut against the sting of tears at the backs of them. Her teeth cut into her bottom lip. Always, except for that one time... With a resolute sniff, she gathered the lines and directed the mare into the street.

Toffee automatically slowed as she approached their farm. Though it was getting dark, there were shouts and laughter as her younger siblings played in the yard. Sarah's hands twitched on the reins when she recognized Anne as one of them. Anne seldom played outside. Yet today, Anne's first day of school when she'd chosen not to go with Sarah, she was. Sarah put a hand to her suddenly twisting stomach. Had she unintentionally been holding Anne back?

The mare balked when, instead of turning into the lane, Sarah urged her to a faster speed. Though Toffee's ears were back in protest, she finally responded. As the buggy continued down the road and passed the far side of the barn, Sarah saw another of her younger sisters at the calf huts, feeding calves that had been weaned from their mothers.

Cupping her hands around her mouth, she called, "Tell *Mamm* I'm going to a friend's house! Don't wait to eat supper! I'll be home later!"

Her sister waved in acknowledgment.

Sarah drew in a deep breath. There was only one friend she had in mind. She worried the inside of her cheek as she prodded the reluctant mare on. Hopefully he was home. She scowled, thinking about Dorothy's sparkling eyes and blush. Home. And alone.

Chapter Seven

Sarah's rigid shoulders relaxed as she turned into the lane. No silhouettes of a horse and buggy were visible at the hitching post next to Gideon's yard. And there was a dark shadow of his mare in the small pen next to the barn. Her mood instantly lightened. This wasn't a foolish errand. It was a reasonable visit to a good friend. Who was thankfully home. And alone. Gideon had information she wanted. Besides, she needed to tell him about Dorothy's appreciation. She might forget about it by Monday.

Ha. Appreciation. That was too tame a word. Her friend was spilling over with admiration for Gideon. For his rescue. For him... Sarah scowled, feeling a companionship with the unhappy mare that was drawing to a halt in front of the hitching post. If she was capable, she'd have flicked her ears back too.

Gideon stepped out onto the porch as she was securing Toffee to the post. "This is...a bit of a surprise. Is everything all right?"

"Ja," she assured him as she headed over the stone pavers to the house.

He looked behind her as if expecting someone else to descend from the buggy. With a furrowed brow, he opened the door for her. "Just couldn't do without more of my company, huh."

"Something like that." Sarah stopped a few feet into the small kitchen. Now that she was here, another case of nerves rippled through her. She curled her hands into her skirt to dry suddenly damp palms. Although she'd been here many times with Ben before her brother had married, this was the first time she'd visited Gideon on her own. It felt…different.

She almost jumped when Gideon pulled the door shut with a soft *click*. He crossed to the table where Sarah could see he'd been refilling oil lamps, a common chore.

"Your family know where you are?" Having apparently finished the task before she arrived, he carried the bottle of paraffin oil to the cupboard where he squatted down and stored it on a lower shelf.

"*Ja*. I told one of my sisters to tell *Mamm* I was going to a friend's place, which is what I did." The last came out a bit defensively. She crossed her arms over her chest. *So get to the reason you came.* "Anne will probably be wondering where I am and wanting to tell me about her day." *At least I hope so, since she wouldn't confide in me earlier today.* "I understand there was a bit of a…hiccup in it."

Gideon returned to the table to wipe down the two lamps there with a cloth. "A hiccup? You mean a hiccup like her running away from school and me finding her in the woods?"

Sarah's heart rate accelerated as she tried to calculate the distance. With studied nonchalance, she leaned back against the counter. "That would be a good place to start. How far did she get?"

He cocked his head as he considered. "About a mile."

A mile! Had Anne ever walked that far before? "Did

she tell you why she ran away? Dorothy said she was all right. But…was she?"

He answered her second question with a seriousness that matched her tone. "I think so. Seemed fine when I let her drive the team back to the school. She likes working with horses, you know."

Leaving one lamp on the kitchen table, he carried the other into the dark common room. Sarah watched him through the kitchen doorway as he set it on an end table next to a mission-style Morris chair. She worried her bottom lip. No, she hadn't known.

Returning to the kitchen, Gideon passed her to open the refrigerator door and peer inside. "I was just about to eat. Are you hungry?"

"What do you have?" Maybe hunger was why her stomach was knotted like tangled yarn.

"Hmm. Let me see what's been brought over." He pulled a few containers out of the refrigerator. As he was doing so, Sarah spied the contents of the gas-powered appliance. At least one full pie and another partial were on the shelves, along with a few containers, the types Amish women used when they were transporting food. There were names marked on them, but though she narrowed her eyes, Sarah couldn't read the lettering before the door swung shut.

Her gaze followed Gideon to the counter where he began opening the containers. She noted a loaf of bread on the counter, perfectly shaped and browned, in a clear plastic baggie. Waspishly, Sarah wondered how many loaves were rejected before this one was chosen. Or—her shoulders sagged—did every loaf the unknown baker make turn out perfect?

She could understand why the unknown girl made the effort. Gideon was a prize. He even had his own place.

Young men were discouraged from marrying unless they had some small parcel of land. They weren't like the *Englisch* who could be satisfied with a garage or street parking. Their horses, which they used for transportation, and the fact many families had a cow required more room than that. Gideon had it all—a home, a solid job, good looks and a charming personality when he chose to employ it. No wonder all the single girls were chasing him. For some reason, the thought made her scowl. An expression she quickly amended when Gideon looked in her direction.

He arched an eyebrow. "Get a couple of bowls out of the cupboard if you would." Sarah turned to do as he suggested, but froze at his next words. "Looks like we're having soup."

He retrieved a pot from the lower cupboard and set it on the stove with a muted *bang*. Sarah heard a gurgling splash and watched from the corner of her eye as he poured what looked like chicken noodle soup into it. Drawing in a slow deep breath, she opened an upper cupboard door, pulled down a dish and took it over to the table with careful steps.

Gideon turned from the stove and frowned. "Only one bowl? You're welcome to join me. It may not be up to your standards, but I'll share."

Sarah wrapped her arms about her torso in a tight hug. "I don't eat soup."

"What? Afraid you'll find someone who's a better cook than you?" His smile was teasing. "That's right, you don't cook." He slid open a drawer, withdrew a tablespoon, sampled the pot's contents and wrinkled his nose. "Well, don't worry, this one isn't much of a cook either."

Sarah licked dry lips. "I don't eat soup even at home."

Gideon swung his head around in exaggerated surprise and opened his mouth. Sarah shrank back, bracing herself for another teasing comment. He regarded her for a moment. Then he closed his mouth and turned to give her his full attention. "How have you avoided soup all these years?"

She swallowed past what felt like the counter's loaf of bread in her throat. "When we have soup at our house, I have a church spread sandwich." She hunched a shoulder. "Or if I'm anywhere else, I just say I'm not hungry."

Gideon firmed his lips as he watched her. Without taking his gaze off her, he reached over to turn off the burner under the pot. "Why don't you eat soup, Sarah?"

"Because…" The backs of her eyes stung. "Because…" She inhaled shakily as she rubbed her hand across her nose to stop its prickling.

"Because I was making soup when Anne was burned." Where were these words coming from? She'd never spoken them before. She tried to keep her breathing steady but she began to pant. "When I see soup, particularly chicken soup, all I can see is…is Anne screaming as she's drenched in it."

She tasted salt. Tears were running down her cheeks to seep into the corner of her mouth. "It was soup that burned her. Soup that took her from being such a happy, beautiful child. And it was…all my fault." The last words burst from her in a wail.

Sarah turned her back to scrub her hands over her wet, heated cheeks. She couldn't bear to have Gideon see her like this. She wanted him to think she was strong. Capable. But right now, her elbows were pressed so tightly against her sides, she was surprised they didn't crack with her violent shaking. Footsteps crossed the linoleum to stop behind her. Sarah grimaced. Ducking her head, she tried to make herself even smaller as she fought for breath through ragged hitches.

She had never told anyone about her aversion to soup. Her family knew it, of course, though she'd never voiced how the sight of a boiling pot of it affected her. She squeezed her eyes shut, but her efforts did nothing to stop the streaming tears. *Gideon must think I'm a fool.* Her churning stomach almost erupted at the prospect of losing his friendship and respect.

If she hadn't already been shaking so hard, she would have jumped when warm arms closed about her. But they did so with such tender strength that her initial stiffness as they carefully encircled her slowly subsided. She sank into their inviting warmth. Gideon gently turned her so her cheek rested against the soft broadcloth of his shirt. She wheezed in a breath filled with the comforting scents of laundry and clean male, mixed with a hint of wood and horse. The heart under her ear beat in a steady rhythm.

There was strength in the chest against her cheek. In the hands that clasped her back. But more than that, there was gentleness. Security. Sarah collapsed into it and sobbed as she hadn't since that horrible day. Instead of putting her away from him as she soaked his shirt with tears, Gideon drew her closer.

As the wracking sobs continued, he began to rock her consolingly. Her wails slowly subsided. Amid the ragged panting, Sarah managed a long, quiet breath. Then two, then three. She sniffed against his damp shirt, aghast to discover the effort did little to stifle her streaming nose. She shifted to lift her head but when he cupped a hand under her *kapp* at the back of her neck and tenderly held her in place, she drooped with exhaustion against his chest.

He continued to rock her. A gentle motion accompanied with soothing murmurs.

"Shhhh. I have you. It's all right."

How long had it been since someone had rocked her? She subsided farther into the safety and support of his arms. She didn't know if her legs—currently the strength of a damp washcloth—would support her if she didn't. There was a soft pressure on the top of her *kapp*, one that reminded her of the rare occasions her *mamm* had kissed her head when she'd been a child. The thought almost made her smile. Surely it was just her imagination. This was, after all, not her *mamm,* but Gideon.

Gideon, her friend, whose shirt she'd just drenched with her tears, running nose and open-mouth blubbering. Her ears began to grow hot with embarrassment. She knew that when she lifted her head, their red appearance would match her face and eyes. Sarah almost groaned. She was tempted to continue hiding in his damp shirt just to avoid facing him. Instead, forcing a crooked smile, she leaned away. This time, Gideon eased his hold, his hands shifting from her back to cup her shoulders.

Their gazes met. Sarah didn't even want to think about what she must look like. Her lips felt as thick and blubbery as curdled milk, her hair, damp from her emotions, her *kapp* smashed on one side, her face… *Ach*, for sure and certain, he'd never seen her looking so awful. Managing a hard swallow, she rolled her eyes.

"I won't cook for you. But I suppose I owe you a laundered shirt."

"You don't owe me anything, Sarah." His eyes were as solemn as his tone.

"Not even an explanation for sobbing all over you?"

He shook his head.

She took a step back. His arms slowly dropped from about her. Sarah was immediately colder without them. She crossed her own over her chest. "I suppose, since you suffered the sobbing, I might as well give you one." She pulled out one of the kitchen chairs and sank onto it.

Chapter Eight

Gideon reached behind him to yank a faded dish towel off the oven handle. He pulled out a chair and handed the towel to Sarah over the table as he sat down. She took it with a limp smile and mopped her face. Now that she was seated, she was tempted to stand again so she could pace the small kitchen as she related what she'd never before told. Briefly tensing to rise, she sagged back into her seat and rested her elbows on the table. After her unexpected crying jag, she didn't have the energy.

Where to begin, on this event that changed my sister's life. And mine as well. Sarah drew in a deep breath and exhaled it with equal slowness. "Anne was such a happy, curious child." Her voice quavered at the memory. She cleared her throat. "All smiles. And so quick. *Mamm* said of all of us, even the older boys, Anne was the quickest to roll over, the quickest to scooch, to crawl, to walk. She was always on the go. Climbing up on chairs. If you looked away for even a moment, you'd find her hanging from the lower window ledges so she could see outside. She'd climb up on anything within reach." Sarah rubbed her temples where a headache was beginning to pound.

"*Mamm* was getting...older when she had Wayne."

Gideon's brows furrowed when she paused. "He's the youngest, *ja*?"

Sarah nodded wearily. "The only one after Anne." She sighed heavily. "*Mamm* was…tired. It had been a hard birth. She wasn't doing…that well. Since I was the oldest girl, most of the house chores came to me. My younger sisters helped of course, but I felt the responsibility to take care of things." Her lips tilted mockingly. "I guess I can get a little carried away sometimes about taking on responsibility."

Gideon smiled faintly. "Now, why doesn't it shock me to hear that."

"I was fixing supper. My younger sisters were pulling weeds in the garden. The boys were helping with the chores. Anne was with me. I kept having to step around her. She'd been walking for a few months. She loved to climb on this stool we had in the kitchen that us younger ones used to reach items in the top cupboard shelves.

"I was making…" Her mouth was so dry it was a wonder she could talk. No surprise after all the tears. She worked up enough moisture to continue. "Chicken soup. I'd put the noodles in. They were boiling. I was cutting bread, hoping *Mamm* would be able to rest for a little while longer. I remember being…proud—" she cringed on the word "—of taking care of everything so well. Of everyone in the house depending on me while she recovered. Of even taking care of her. Wayne was a colicky baby, but he and *Mamm* were finally sleeping in her bedroom."

Her head dropped forward. Pins securing her *kapp* shifted as some strands of hair slipped loose from it. "But he started to cry. I rushed in there to get him. I didn't want him to wake *Mamm*. I brought him out and was trying to settle him back down by walking with him in the common room." She reached up to wipe a tear from the corner of her eye and dispassionately regarded the drop on her fingertip. *How can I have any tears left?* Her lips started to tremble.

Gideon reached across the table and took her hand. After a moment's hesitation, she clutched it gratefully. "I heard a crash. Followed by horrible screaming." Sarah closed her eyes and let the tears leak from them unheeded. She flinched when something gently brushed against her cheek. Popping her eyes open, she saw Gideon was tenderly dabbing at her tears with the dish towel in his free hand.

"She was on the stool. She must have pushed it over to the stove. There was a puddle of soup under her, the pot lying a few feet away. Noodles and bits of carrots clung to her. Her skin was all red. She was screaming. I won't ever forget her screaming." Her air escaped in a shudder. "And it was my fault. I was supposed to be watching her."

She risked meeting Gideon's eyes, prepared to see the judgment there. There was none in the blue depths. Only compassion. And…sorrow. For her? He didn't speak, only waited for her to continue.

She drew in a deep breath. "*Mamm* came rushing out of the bedroom. I thrust the baby at her and ran to Anne. I raced with her into the bathroom and started pouring cold water over her. She kept screaming. Finally the screams subsided to whimpers. The other girls were drawn to the house with all the noise. *Mamm* told them to have *Daed* harness the horse. They took Anne into the doctor. I stayed home with the others. I cleaned up the mess. I found something for everyone to have for supper, though no one felt like eating."

Sarah released Gideon's hand, surprised at how reluctant she was to do so. She leaned back in her chair. "Baby Wayne couldn't be in the hospital, so *Mamm* needed to be at home with him. I stayed in the hospital with Anne over the next week while they treated the burns. They were deep.

By the time we came home, Leah and my other younger sisters had taken over the cooking." She shook her head slowly. "*Mamm* never blamed me. Never said anything about me cooking again." She smiled feebly. "Nor made me eat soup after that. And chicken noodle soup is never fixed at our house."

"It was an accident."

She continued to numbly shake her head. "I should have been watching her more closely. I was in charge. I was responsible." She was so tired. Crossing her arms on the table, she rested her head on them and closed her eyes. She felt like she'd been through their gas-powered washing machine—stirred hard in the tub and squeezed through the finger-pinching wringer.

But for all that, she also felt lighter. *Maybe after going through the wringer I'm now hung on the line to blow with the breeze.*

If so, it was a gentle breeze. The kitchen was quiet, other than the scrape of Gideon's chair as he pushed it back from the table. Wearily, she opened her eyes and watched him stand to cross to the counter, where a lumpy splash sounded again as he poured the soup from the pot back into the container and sealed it.

"I don't think I'm hungry for soup either." He didn't bother to put the soup back into the refrigerator, instead leaving it on the counter as he perused the fridge's contents. Sarah wondered idly if the soup's fate was to feed the pair of pigs Gideon was raising to butcher. Her lips twitched. How sad the hopeful cook would be if she knew that was where her careful preparation had gone. Sarah doubted the way to a man's heart was through the hog lot, but with Gideon, who knew? The prospect prompted a genuine smile when she'd doubted she'd be capable of one for some time.

"You feel like pie?"

Sarah sat up and pressed a hand to her stomach. Surprisingly, she might. "What kind?"

Gideon stuck his head back into the refrigerator. "Looks like pumpkin and…" There was a rattle as something was opened. "Pecan."

She cocked her head. "Do you have whipped cream?"

More rattling sounded as some refrigerator's contents were shifted around. "Doesn't look like it."

"Who would bring over pumpkin pie without whipped cream? Unless they thought you'd make some?"

He raised his head above the open door to cock an eyebrow at her. "Do I look like I'd make whipped cream? I don't even have a cow. Any milk I need I get from my sister or sisters-in-law and I'm not about to ask for whipped cream and admit to them that other women are making me pies. They might stop making an occasional one for me themselves." He grinned a Gideon grin. And Sarah knew that even though she'd made a total fool of herself in front of him, it was going to be all right.

"Pecan, then."

Gideon watched as Sarah rose from her chair to retrieve a couple of plates from the cupboard. He sighed quietly in relief. He hadn't known the details of Anne's accident. And that was what it was, an accident. Yes, it could have been avoided. But it also could have been any of her sisters or even Anne's mother in the kitchen when Wayne started crying. All of whom might have hurried to attend the baby, never expecting the toddler to be so quick.

And now that he did know the details…he ached for Sarah. He ached for them both. And he understood better where Sarah's protective attitude toward her younger sister came from.

She carried the plates to the table and sat down. "Are you going to tell me who made the pie?"

"No." He shut the refrigerator door, removed the pie from its container and brought it to the table, returning a moment later with a knife and two forks before dropping onto the chair across from her. He cut two large slices, slid them onto the plates and shoved one and a fork in her direction.

"Because then you'd probably say something to her and she might stop making them for me. And she might be a *gut* cook, which…" He took a bite of the pie and tilted his head back and forth. "She's not bad." He took another forkful and spoke around it. "She might even get really *gut* over a few more pies."

Sarah rolled her eyes and shook her own head as she cut a small piece from her slice and ate it. Her eyes narrowed as she carefully chewed and swallowed. "It's not from Dorothy, is it?"

"*Nee.* What with getting settled in at school and such, I doubt she's had time to make me a pie. Yet." He swung his leg to the side, avoiding Sarah's attempted kick under the table.

"She stopped by the shop looking for you this afternoon. I'm supposed to thank you for rescuing her today." Sarah batted her eyes in pretend flirtation before grimacing. "I shouldn't mock her like that. She's sweet and is becoming a friend. Hopefully a good one. One I'm glad to have with everyone else getting married. Still, to help her feel more welcome…" She cut another morsel of pie and looked at him from under her eyelashes. "Maybe you could talk with some of your single friends. Have someone ask to take her home after a singing."

"I don't think much talking needs to be involved. She's a pretty girl and, as you say, sweet. Probably before long, Isaiah will be looking for a new schoolteacher again."

Sarah smiled but her eyes clouded a bit at his prediction. She set down her fork and leaned back. "The rescue was apparently for bringing Anne back. You never answered if she told you why she ran away today."

Gideon purposely stuffed in a big bite and took his time chewing it. How much should he tell her? There was no doubt she was an advocate for Anne and knowing what was affecting her sister might help Anne adjust. "There was apparently a boy in school who teased her about her scars."

Sarah scowled and half rose out of her chair.

"I don't think Lily will let anyone bother Anne within her hearing. The teaser is a boy who's the youngest in his family. Probably gets bullied at home and thinks he's finally found someone weaker than him. She isn't, you know. I think, once she gains a bit of confidence, she'll work it out on her own, somehow, some way." Taking the final bite of pie—which really wasn't bad at all—he leveled a gaze at Sarah until she settled back onto her seat.

She did so with a huff. "What makes you an expert?"

"I was a younger brother. Still am. We want to prove ourselves. It's difficult to do with…powerful older brothers."

She frowned. "I can't see Malachi bullying you when you were a child."

"You're right." He grinned. "It was mainly Samuel. But Malachi bossed me around in his own way. A little more tactfully, true." Gideon pushed his plate off to the side and rested his elbows on the table. "And still does." He sighed and continued when confronted with her furrowed brow. "This job. Or my current job, anyway. I never asked for it. I don't want it. I was planning to—" His mouth snapped shut.

"Planning to what?"

"*Ach*, not planning to do what I'm currently doing. And now he wants me to hire somebody. Get them up to speed so when the new warehouse is ready, so are they. What do I know about hiring? I've never done anything like that before."

Sarah pushed her own plate aside and smiled. "It could be because he trusts you."

Gideon rubbed a hand over his mouth. "Well, maybe he shouldn't."

"Do you have anyone in mind?"

"I've put out some feelers." He lurched off the chair and carried their plates to the counter. When he turned back to the table, Sarah was rising to her feet.

"I should be going. It's gotten late."

Though he'd been startled and a bit apprehensive at her solo arrival, Gideon was surprised at the overwhelming urge to convince her to stay longer. Having her here had been… He couldn't find an appropriate word, only knew that the rest of the evening and those going forward would be missing something.

"I also need to thank you." She pushed in her chair. "For bringing Anne safely back when she was upset and ran away and…" her smile wobbled a bit "…for being such a good friend."

When Gideon looked at her across the table, her eyes red, her cheeks a bit splotchy, her nose shining, her hair coming down from her *kapp*—friendship wasn't what came to mind. What did was…tenderness…joy…love?

Gideon slumped against the counter. Whoa. He'd figured whenever he grew to…care for someone—and he'd hoped someday he would—that he'd have the relationship his siblings had with their spouses. He'd never expected the moment to hit him when his shirt was still wet from her tears. He'd always had an eye for a pretty woman. And the moment he fell for someone, she looked like she was allergic to chickens and had just spent a week in a crowded henhouse.

So what did one do when they realized they were in love? Particularly with someone who'd just thanked them for being a good friend? *Ach*, for sure and certain, they didn't rush across the kitchen, sweep the girl into their arms and kiss her like there was no tomorrow. Though the thought did briefly cross his mind. Instead, at least for the time being, he would act like a friend.

There were two reasons she'd thanked him. Both related in some way to Anne. Gideon drew in a deep breath. Should he tell her the whole of it? Tell her what prompted Anne's decision to go to school today? If you had information on something of importance to someone you cared for, should you tell them? He scowled. Being in love was already a complicated and heavy responsibility.

"Why are you looking at me like that?"

Gideon shook his head. If he was in her situation, would he want to know? Straightening from the counter, he sighed and curled his hand into a fist. What if he was wrong?

"The reason Anne didn't want to come into the shop with you this morning is because she thinks you're embarrassed of her." His stomach knotted as he watched Sarah's face turn white. It tightened further at the white in the knuckles of the hands that reached out to grip the back of the kitchen chair. He slapped his arms over his chest, wishing he could kick himself. Or have one of the Belgians do it. Two minutes into determining he loved a woman and he'd already broken her heart.

"Oh no! Never embarrassed! Why would she think that?"

"She understood some of what you and the *Englischer*

were talking of yesterday. She thinks you want her to have more surgeries because you're embarrassed of her scars."

"Oh no! I wanted them for her because I... I thought she'd want them to make the scars less visible. Less obvious. So she's not teased about them like she was at school today."

Gideon winced when tears again leaked down her cheeks. "I told her it wasn't true. That you care very deeply for her."

Sarah nodded mutely. Her lips trembled. Tears dripped off her chin to fall on the pinned front of her dress.

Gideon couldn't stand it anymore. He opened his arms. "Oh, come here. My shirt's already wet."

She stumbled around the table to him and did so, soaking his shirt anew. He wrapped his arms about her. This wasn't the way he wanted her in them, but having her there still felt like he was holding a missing piece of himself.

"I'm sorry. I didn't tell you to make you cry." He sighed. "I thought you might like to know. I know I would." Gideon rested his chin on her head and stared at his white-painted cupboards. He had a few secrets of his own that his brother might like to, or deserved to, know.

"Why didn't she tell me herself?" The words were mumbled into his shirt.

"Maybe she thought you'd be disappointed in her?"

Sarah shook her head. "Never."

"Don't tell her I told you. I don't want to lose her trust, but I thought it might help you to understand her actions."

"She doesn't want another surgery?"

"No. Or at least not right now."

"But surely she wants the scars to go away as much as possible?"

"She does? Or you do? Because you feel responsible."

She was quiet for a moment before whispering, "I am responsible."

Gideon put his hands on her shoulders and pulled her back until he could meet her eyes. "Sarah. It was an accident. It could have happened with any one of your family."

"But I was the one who was there. Now I have to make it as right as I can."

"Sometimes we can't undo what's been done. We just have to make the best of what is."

She took a step back and swiped the back of her hand under her eyes. Gideon released her shoulders, snagged the dish towel that was still on the table and handed it to her.

"*Denki* for telling me. I promise I won't blab to her what you said. But it does give me something to think about. Well…" Her gaze lifted to the clock on the wall behind him. "I do need to be going. I'll see you on Monday." She headed for the door.

Gideon followed her. "The temperature has dropped. Though it took its time, looks like fall has finally arrived. Do you want a coat? It'll keep you a lot warmer than a damp dish towel."

Sarah glanced at the limp cloth she clutched in her hand. With a grimace, she tossed it onto the table. "*Nee*. I have a blanket in the buggy."

She looked so woebegone. Gideon kept his arms to his side though he longed to reach out to her again. "Are you going to be all right going home?"

"*Ja*. Even if I weep on the journey, Toffee knows the way home and will be pretty eager to get there."

Gideon followed her out to the buggy and waited while she climbed in and retrieved a blanket from the back. He watched as she drove out the lane, realizing as she turned onto the road that he was rubbing his hand over where her tears had wet his shirt. Over his heart.

Why hadn't he left a month ago? Before he knew of the warehouse. Before Malachi's dependence on him. Before his feelings for Sarah went from friendship to love. How was he going to leave her now? Because for sure and certain, she'd never leave her family and he couldn't ask her to choose between him and them. But could he stay and give up his own dreams?

He headed up the walk. He still didn't know if it had been the right thing to tell Sarah about Anne's feelings. But if it was the right thing to be honest with someone you cared about when you knew something that affected them, wasn't it time he told Malachi of his own feelings?

Chapter Nine

"This isn't like milking a cow. If you're not paying attention all the time, you might lose a finger. Or worse." Gideon almost rolled his eyes at his own words. *I sound like Malachi when he was teaching me so many years ago.*

His shoulders tensed. *Malachi, who I need to talk with today.* He'd almost headed over to his brother's place on Visiting Sunday to finally share his dreams and plans to explore a new job and location but had changed his mind on his way out to harness Jazz. What if Malachi and Ruth had company? It was probably better to leave business discussions at business. But with him busy at this shop and Malachi spending almost all his time at the other location, he hadn't had a chance yet. He twisted his lips. And maybe he was still procrastinating, as here it was a week from when he'd determined to tell him.

"Things might not be quite as soft as a cow, but they do smell better. And cleaning up after them should be a little more pleasant." Josiah Lapp grinned as he followed Gideon around the varied equipment in the shop.

"I'm serious, Josiah. You need to be paying attention to what you're doing all the time. Some of this might seem like monotonous work, but your mind can't wander. You can't be daydreaming of the girl you brought home from the last singing or the one you want to bring home from the next one. You're working around dangerous equipment."

Gideon grimaced. He was a fine one to talk. Ever since last Friday, when he'd realized his feelings for Sarah were much more than friendship, he'd either been thinking of her or making some excuse to step into the office and see her. Even now, with the image of her popping into his head, he was remembering the feel of her in his arms, the honeysuckle scent of her hair and the overwhelming desire to share her burdens.

Anne hadn't returned to the shop. When he asked Sarah how things were going for her sister at school, she'd shared that something seemed to be bothering Anne there, but her friendship with Lily had been a help. Sarah had also assured him that he'd made the right choice in telling her about Anne's reluctance for more surgeries, which had relieved him greatly. Though she'd smiled when she told him, Gideon could tell Sarah was still hurt that Anne hadn't confided in her.

Considering his wary decision to have a conversation with Malachi, Gideon understood Anne's sentiment. It was hard to talk with someone you cared for when you were worried about hurting or disappointing them.

Sarah's cheeks had been a little rosy when she'd first come in on Monday and found him in the office. Residue, he was sure, of embarrassment over her crying jag Friday night. He'd teased her about not being able to dry his dishes and almost not coming to work because he didn't get his soggy dishtowel and shirt laundered. She'd teased him back about his diet of pies and wondered what was on his menu for this week. And then they were back to normal. At least she was. He was far from normal. Wasn't sure he even wanted the "old" normal. And was apprehensive about suggesting a new one. What if Sarah preferred the old one?

"What's next?"

Gideon jolted back to the noise of saws, belt sanders and other equipment run by a rumbling generator in an adjoining shed. Josiah was eyeing him expectantly. Jerking into motion, Gideon continued to the back of the shop to stop in front of a waist-high piece of equipment with a large flat surface extending a short distance in both directions.

"Have you used a planer before?"

"Seen one. Haven't used one."

"Along with milling and squaring up rough lumber, it also reduces the thickness of boards. The hand wheel sets the height accordingly." Gideon selected a board from the nearby stack and did so. "You'll know it's set properly when the in-feed rollers start pulling the piece into the machine." He turned on the planer and demonstrated. When the board, with a smoother surface, came out the other side, he handed it to Josiah and turned off the machine.

"Watch out for knots on the wood. When the cutter head hits those, it can jolt the board like a bucking horse and if you get hit with it, it feels like a mule kick."

At Josiah's nod, Gideon moved to the next piece of equipment. Despite Josiah's jokes as Gideon gave the new employee a brief overview of the equipment and workshop, the man's eyes were intent on whatever Gideon was demonstrating and the questions he asked were relevant and insightful.

"Before we turn you loose on any of these, you'll do everything under supervision. But you'll start out on the tedious, low-skill jobs. You might be there a while, depending on how quickly you learn. Are you sure you don't want to go back to the cows?"

Josiah shook his head, his expression surprisingly serious. "There's no future for me on the farm. Not one that could support a family anyway. Harley will take over when *Daed* decides to slow down and as youngest son, he'll eventually inherit it. I do like the cows, and there's always plenty of work there. I'll certainly help after hours. But I'd prefer learning another trade. Even though the area is growing, there're still not a lot of opportunities around close for young men when there are getting to be such an abundance of us." His face creased in a wide grin. "So thanks for hiring me."

"Don't thank me yet. You might not like it."

Josiah looked around the well-organized workshop at the equipment and works in progress. "Oh, I think I will. I'm ready to try something new. And as I mentioned, it smells a bit better than what I'm used to and I don't have to watch what I step in."

Gideon took in the shop as well. A place that had been a second home for him for several years. He swallowed past a surprising lump that had suddenly appeared in his throat. "I admit I am a bit shocked to hear the words, and concerns, of 'supporting a family' coming from you. Is there going to be an announcement soon in church regarding an upcoming wedding?"

He raised his eyebrows at the blush that spread up Josiah's neck and into his cheeks. The younger man gave his head a quick, hard shake. "*Nee.* It just makes sense to be thinking about a long-term and secure way of making a living."

"With the new warehouse, there'll be plenty of opportunity here." Gideon led Josiah over to where Ben was working and left his friend to show Schrock Brothers Furniture's newest addition the finer points of hand-sanding as they wrapped up the workday.

Despite his experience being more in carpentry than woodworking, Josiah was a quick study. Gideon had worked with him on community projects and knew the teasing young man to be surprisingly meticulous. He'd do a good job. He hoped. Gideon blew out a breath. This was the first time he'd hired and trained someone. What did he know about any of it? Malachi had told him to bring someone in and do it as promptly as possible. So he had.

As he walked back up through the workstations, his gaze landed on a large drawer, one of several, in a clear, hard plastic cabinet. Gideon frowned and strode over to investigate. He pulled the drawer out and stirred the contents with a finger. They were running low on washers, a surprisingly crucial component of furniture building. Gideon grabbed one of the inventory sheets he kept pinned to a nearby bulletin board. With a seasoned eye, he did a quick inventory, something he hadn't yet done this week, on the basic fasteners that kept the shop running.

Sheet in hand, he entered the showroom. As had become his custom, he did a swift scan, locating Sarah where she was busy with a customer at the front of the store. With a small sigh that she wasn't free for a chat, Gideon turned to the office, only to stop abruptly in the doorway when he saw Malachi working at the desk.

His heart started to pound. Here was his opportunity. He'd wanted to catch his brother alone and at work, and here he was.

His mouth suddenly dried up, as well as any appropriate words necessary to start the difficult topic. He should have been practicing this conversation, in his head if not out loud. But practicing would have made the situation more real. More imminent. More permanent. What if Malachi didn't take it well? What would that do to their working relationship here? Would he then be forced to leave as it was no longer comfortable working in the shop? Or was he not being fair to his brother? Malachi was pretty reasonable.

Gideon shifted back a step. Where he'd been certain before that he was leaving, now—with his newfound feelings for Sarah—he wasn't so sure. Still, it was only fair to tell Malachi what he was thinking. He couldn't put it off forever. He cleared his throat.

"I didn't know you were coming in today." Gideon was startled at the hoarseness in his voice.

Malachi didn't look up from his work. "I ran into a few things I needed some information on."

Gideon stepped into the office. "Well, since you're here, there's been something I've been meaning to...to mention to you."

Malachi, wearing an uncustomary frown, lifted his gaze. He nodded to the door behind Gideon, the one that was always open. With a furrowed brow, Gideon shut it with a quiet *click*.

"Is it regarding your new hire? Josiah? Surely there were some more...mature candidates available."

Gideon felt like he'd been punched in the midsection. The fact that his stomach was already roiling with tension didn't help. "Josiah's a good worker."

"When he's not chasing girls."

"I don't think that will be a problem. Granted, Josiah likes to flirt. But there aren't any girls here to chase." Other than the one in the office. Gideon's gut twisted further at the realization.

"I'm still surprised at your choice."

"You told me to get someone hired." Gideon fisted his hands, crinkling the paper he held.

"Someone who can do the job."

"He can do the job." His voice was as sharp as the edge of one of the 2x4 boards in the workshop. "Besides, he's here now. You wanted someone in as quickly as possible. I can't go back and retract the job offer. If that's what you want, you can do it yourself. In fact, if you don't like who I brought in, you should have done it yourself and made your own choice."

Malachi leaned back in the office chair. "It's not that I don't like Josiah." He grimaced. "He's a very likable guy. Comes from a *gut* family. His brother Jonah's been a tremendous help at the warehouse. But I need someone who can be ready when we get the new warehouse going. And I don't know that he's it."

"And when will that be? When will the warehouse be up and running?" Gideon bit off the words. He'd never been so frustrated with his brother. He'd done the job he was asked to do, a job he hadn't wanted, and now he was being chastised for it.

Malachi rubbed a hand across his face. "Not as soon as I'd hoped. I *know* the purchase is still a *gut* decision. But some of the costs on getting it up and running are going to be higher than I expected. And extended equipment lead times…" He shook his head, his mouth a grim line. "It's going to take longer than I expected. Be more expensive than I expected."

Gideon glanced down at the paper in his hand, the now wrinkled list of different nails, screws, bolts, nuts and washers. It seemed like every one of them was securing him to this job, in a place where his work was unappreciated and pulling him away from his own dreams.

"How long do you anticipate?" Gideon's voice was as flat as boards coming off the planer.

"Before the equipment all gets in and we're up and running at the new location or before there's a hundred percent return on investment?"

"Before it's up and running and you've got everything moved out of here." *The ROI isn't a concern for me. I'm not going to be around to see it.*

Malachi gave him a distracted smile before he dropped his attention to the paperwork in front of him. "It'll be a bit. Don't worry, little brother. You'll have a chance to do more effective hiring."

"Not me," Gideon muttered as he jerked open the door. Sarah was in his line of sight at the counter. Upon seeing him, she grinned. Though his heart lurched, Gideon gave her a brief nod in return and exited into the workshop. He left shortly after with the rest of the men.

He was still irritated while doing chores that evening. Even the effort of throwing down an additional week's hay from the loft hadn't worked it out of him. *I didn't ask for this job. I definitely didn't ask to do your hiring for you. It's a small community. If you had such strong opinions, you should have told me who you wanted. Or who you wanted to avoid. And now I question my own judgment.* He gritted his teeth. *But I know Josiah can do the job. If you want him fired, you'll have to do it yourself.*

Gideon stomped down the lane to get the mail. Jerking open the battered metal door, he scowled at the lone envelope inside. Just what he needed tonight, an unexpected bill. When he pulled the envelope out, his brow furrowed at the unfamiliar name on the return address. As his gaze dropped to the town and state, he sucked in a breath. Joseph

Brenneman was the bishop of a small Amish settlement in Crook County in northeastern Wyoming. He'd written the man weeks ago—before he'd learned of Malachi's expansion—explaining his background and wondering if they might have a place in their community for his talents.

He tapped the envelope a few times against his palm. If it was a rejection, he didn't know if he was prepared to handle it today. His fingers tightened on the corner, indenting the paper. But what if the bishop was saying yes? Did he still want to go now that he wanted something beyond a friendship with Sarah?

But this might be his opportunity to see—to more than see, to experience—the West. While Ohio and Wisconsin had been *wunderbar*, there was something about the prospect of wide-open spaces, mountains in the distance and the mystique of the West that called to him. Although it would be an adjustment, knowing there was only a small Amish population in Wyoming, not much more than five hundred, made him feel like a pioneer in settling there. The knowledge that Wyoming itself had a low population density attracted him.

Of course, after a long winter seeing the same handful of folks—and maybe few of them single and female and none of them Sarah—he might not be so attracted. But at least he would have tried. He'd always wonder if he didn't.

Inhaling deeply, he slipped a calloused thumb under the envelope's flap and opened it. It took another deep breath before he pulled out the handwritten sheets—several of them, was that a good sign?—unfolded them and began to read. The bishop's penmanship was surprisingly neat. Even so, Gideon read the pages through twice before dropping his hand and staring unseeing at the small pasture in front of him.

His heart pounded. It was even better than he could have hoped. The bishop explained that Gideon's request had been very timely. Their carriage builder, who'd moved out when the Amish district originally located in the area, was getting older. He wanted to retire and return to the Midwest where most of his family still lived. The man was willing to stay on a bit and teach someone his skills so the community wouldn't lose this valuable resource. He would also give the newcomer priority option on his home, as it was on the same property as the business. A ready-made occupation and place to live. If Gideon was interested.

He certainly was. He slid his hand down the side of his pants to keep from dampening the precious paper. It was exactly the opportunity he was looking for. The district wanted to avoid tourism and the false environment and elevated prices associated with it. The bishop cautioned that living in the West required a person to be tough. Far from dissuading Gideon, the warning excited him. The district's leader noted that Gideon's background sounded like he had several skills that would be assets to the growing community.

It was the last line of the letter that had Gideon's stomach filling with lead. The bishop ended with the admonition that he'd need to hear back promptly, because the buggy maker was eager to retire. If Gideon wasn't interested, they'd offer the opportunity to someone else.

He flipped the mailbox lid closed and rubbed a hand across his mouth as he slowly started up the lane. Yesterday his decision might have been different. Yesterday he might have delayed until he'd finally talked with Malachi about his thoughts on leaving along with a promise to stay for as long as needed to get the new warehouse established.

But yesterday, he'd felt appreciated by his brother.

Today…well, there were other employees who could do the things he'd been doing and probably wouldn't get a closed-door meeting for doing them.

He quickened his pace. He had his own life to live. His own business, one perfectly suited to him, to establish. He didn't have to continually live his brother's life, especially if he wasn't appreciated for doing so.

He burst into the house, set the letter on the table, collected a pen and paper and sat down. As he faced the blank sheet, his energy seeped away.

Yes or no?

A yes to the bishop would be a no to a possible relationship with Sarah. Perhaps even one with his brothers. A no would be denying his dreams and continuing to live someone else's. Was he selfish to want his own?

What if he stayed and Sarah never wanted anything more than friendship? He would have missed this opportunity and gained potential heartache by watching her eventually marry another man.

Malachi would understand, wouldn't he? After all, he'd left home to pursue his dream in another state. There were many capable in Schrock Brothers who could step up. Ben would be a *gut* mentor for Josiah and anyone else Malachi decided to hire.

Gideon frowned at the squiggly pen marks made on the page by his shaking hand. He got a clean piece of paper out, took a deep breath and began to write.

Dear Bishop Brenneman,
I'm happy to accept your offer…

Chapter Ten

With a cupped hand, Sarah swept cheese curls and Fritos from the tabletop into a small trash can. She shook her head. How she'd ever thought the sixteen-year-old and seventeen-year-old boys who tossed them at each other—and at a few girls across the table—during singings were attractive, she didn't know. But then again, she was no longer a sixteen-year-old girl just entering her *rumspringa*.

She paused at the sound of a familiar laugh and looked over to see where Gideon was the center of attention, of men and women, on the far side of the room. She'd about fallen off her chair when he'd walked in earlier that evening. What was he doing here? He rarely attended singings anymore. Not since most of his friends—and hers—had married.

At least he seemed in a better mood than when he'd left work on Friday. Lately, he'd been stopping in the shop at the end of the day and walking with her out to the shed where they hitched up their horses. But though she'd waited, he never came back into the showroom after a rare closed-door meeting with Malachi. She'd peeked into the office to ask if Malachi wanted her to lock up or if he was going to do it. Her boss, usually very friendly, had nodded distractedly and said he'd take care of it.

Had the two had a fight? It seemed impossible. They always got along so well.

She hadn't had a chance to talk with Gideon this morning at church. He'd arrived too late to visit beforehand and after the services she'd been busy helping serve the meals. The weather had finally turned cold, no surprise for November in Wisconsin, and windy to boot, so there were no volleyball games today. The young women had stayed in the house to chat, with the exception of a few flirtatious ones who'd ventured out to the barn where the men had congregated after the meal. She hadn't seen him after that. This evening when he arrived, he'd been swarmed like the lone hive in a county full of honeybees. She'd tried to catch his eye while they'd been singing—well, while the girls had been singing and several of the boys had been pitching corn curls—but when their gazes had met, he'd just given her a brief nod and looked away.

Obviously, something was bothering him. He'd been such a good friend to her when she was upset. She wanted to return the favor. But not in the midst of an eavesdropping crowd.

Sarah slid the last of the debris into the trash can and finished wiping the table. She straightened and, with a hand on her hip, scanned the room. Most of the girls tonight were younger than her. She smiled at Dorothy, who was collecting abandoned drinking glasses from around the room. Sarah and her younger siblings—the two old enough to be in their *rumspringa*—had swung over and picked the schoolteacher up on the way. At least with her friend here, Sarah didn't feel like a budding single sister or a leftover blessing, as the Amish sometimes called their spinsters.

But Gideon had been right when he'd told her Dorothy wouldn't need any help finding a beau. With the glances a few of the men were casting in her friend's direction, the school board president might indeed soon need to search for another teacher. Sarah twisted her lips, her shoulders slumping. Leaving her to be a sidesitter at another *Eck* table and watch another friend get married. And be left behind again.

Disheartened, she trudged across the large kitchen before coming to an abrupt halt, causing one of the other girls helping to bump into her back.

"Sorry." The girl gave her a raised brow as she stepped around her.

Sarah remained rooted to the linoleum, the small trash can clutched in one hand.

She'd brooded on Anne's reluctance to confide in her since Gideon had shared her sister's feelings a week ago. Hearing that Anne thought she was embarrassed of her had hurt. Deeply. She was responsible for the change in her sister's life, and all Sarah had ever wanted was to remedy that —as much as possible. She hadn't told Anne what Gideon had shared, but it had made her more aware of what she said around her sister.

But if Anne truly didn't want any more surgeries… Sarah's heart rate began racing like she'd been running around the farm's acreage instead of singing fast hymns seated at a table. If Anne didn't want any more surgeries, Sarah wouldn't have to contribute to her medical bills. If she didn't have the bills to pay, she wouldn't have to continue working. If she didn't have to continue working… maybe she could allow herself to think of a wedding in her future. And a family.

Sarah looked over her shoulder to where the men congregated. Her gaze immediately sought out the tall one with golden blond hair. One whose embrace was strong, yet infinitely tender. One to whom she'd revealed her deepest guilt. She tore her eyes away before Gideon could catch her staring at him. How he would laugh, and probably run, if he knew she even momentarily thought of him when the words *wedding* and *family* popped into her head. He'd quickly regret how she'd misinterpreted the comfort he'd given her regarding Anne.

Sarah's gaze slid on to land on a dark-haired man who was looking back. A smile crossed his attractive face. Her eyes narrowed. She couldn't immediately recall his name. He'd been introduced as someone's cousin from another district, who'd come to the singing as their Church Sundays were on opposite weekends. That wasn't uncommon. She'd visited other communities where she had friends and relatives on off Sundays herself on occasion. The man wasn't as young as some of the others. He seemed nice. Fun.

She glanced back to Gideon to find him with Dorothy. Her friend was playing with the ribbons of her *kapp* as she talked. Sarah knew the ploy. She'd engaged it a few times herself. But seeing it now, used on Gideon, made her stomach tighten before she pulled her gaze away and again locked eyes with the newcomer, who was still watching her with a lazy grin.

With Gideon and Dorothy solidly in her peripheral vision, Sarah smiled back.

Turning away, she continued to the mudroom to put the small trash can in a narrow supply closet. When she closed the closet door, it was to discover the young man had green eyes to go along with his dark hair and charming smile.

He nodded toward the closet. "Renegade chip duty, huh?"

Sarah laughed. "It's amazing how many of them escape.

I'm Sarah. I don't believe I've seen you at one of our singings before."

"That's because I didn't know that you were attending them."

She raised her eyebrows at the smooth compliment. One accompanied by a wink and a wider smile. "And now that you do?"

"I may have to plan more trips over here."

"Because you like the songs?" Sarah discovered she was fiddling with the strings of her *kapp*. For some reason, the realization bothered her. She lowered her hands to her waist.

"Because I like the singers. And I'd like to get to know them better. Particularly one of them. Do you have a ride home tonight?"

Sarah's brows tented again. He was a fast worker. "If I did, it would be with someone I at least knew the name of."

"That's easy. Jared. My cousin Noah Reihl invited me. So now that you know…?"

She knew his type at least. "Before I make any decisions, I'd need to talk with my siblings to see what their plans are. Unfortunately, the horse isn't going to get back home by itself." She softened the pretext with a smile. Jared didn't need to know her younger brother would drive the rig home, with or without Sarah and her sister in it. In fact, he might prefer without so he could ask to take a girl home himself.

She wasn't even sure she wanted a ride home tonight, other than with her brother. If someone was going to take her home, and she would presumably spend hours with him in the house when everyone else was asleep, it should be someone she really wanted to be with. Given her recent realization of her freedom to do so, she wanted someone who would go from a ride home, to a beau…to a husband. Someone who would be a friend as well as a husband. Although Jared of the wide smile and glinting eyes might be fun, she didn't know if he'd be that person.

But then—as she looked over his shoulder through the doorway to the rest of the room, her gaze landing on Gideon before darting away—she didn't know who was.

"Can you give me a bit of time to let you know?"

Jared's white-toothed grin dimmed. "A bit," he conceded.

"*Denki,* I'll let you know as soon as I can." *As soon as I can come up with an excuse not to go.* "I have to see if the hostess needs my help for anything else. I'll talk with you shortly?" Following a light touch on his arm to ease the dismissal, she hustled to the kitchen to snag a dish towel from the stove handle and strike up a conversation with the home's owner as she dried the few remaining items in the drainer and tried to think of a tactful way to refuse his offer.

Sarah was putting the final glasses into a cupboard when she felt a light tap on her shoulder. She looked over her shoulder at Dorothy. The blonde's eyes were bright over the steepled hands that were pressed to her mouth. An uneasy boding had Sarah crossing her arms over her chest as she turned to fully face the excited woman.

"I want to thank you so much for picking me up tonight. I'm so glad I came. But I won't be needing a ride home." The announcement was accompanied by flushed cheeks and followed by a giggle.

The sound rippled up Sarah's spine. She pressed back until the edge of the counter bit into her hip. If Dorothy didn't need a ride home with her, that meant she had one with someone else. And the only someone else she'd seen her talk with tonight was…Gideon.

"That's…that's *wunderbar.*"

Her friend didn't seem to notice the response was greatly

lacking in enthusiasm. But then, Dorothy exhibited enough for both of them. "I'd never really had a chance to thank Gideon for his help. I was thrilled to see him here tonight. I was hoping he'd ask me sometime, but that he's doing it so soon! I'd squeal with excitement like one of my students if there weren't so many folks around to hear me."

"That's *wunderbar*," Sarah repeated numbly. Her stomach felt like it was filled with the cast-iron skillet that resided on the nearby stove.

Dorothy was practically bouncing on her toes. "I need to get my cloak. He said he's ready to go. But I needed, *nee*, I wanted to tell you. Thanks so much for becoming such a *gut* friend." Dorothy leaned in to give Sarah a quick hug before hurrying away in the direction of the downstairs bedroom where they'd all deposited their coats.

Sarah remained propped up against the counter. *Why do I feel like I'm going to lose anything I might have consumed today? I'm the one who told Gideon to talk with somebody about taking her home after a singing. I just didn't expect it to be...him.* She lifted a hand to press it against her lips. *What difference does it make if it is? He's a friend. Albeit a* good *one, but just a friend.*

But she lost her friends when they got married. And if she lost her female friends, for sure and certain, she'd lose a male friend—if, and when—he married. For Gideon, who had the pick of theirs and the surrounding districts, it would be a when.

Sarah pushed away from the counter and rubbed her hands down her face. When she opened her eyes, it was to meet Gideon's gaze from across the room. He gave her a faint smile and a nod. Sarah dipped her chin in response before abruptly breaking eye contact. There was something in his gaze. She didn't recognize what it was. Only knew it made her...ache.

But maybe now, she wouldn't be left behind again. Sarah firmed her jaw and quickly scanned the crowd. When she strolled across the room to Jared, it was with a subtle swing in her hips.

"Is that offer of a ride still open?"

Chapter Eleven

Gideon hadn't planned on attending the singing tonight, but he couldn't stay away. His response to Bishop Brenneman had gone out yesterday. He'd marched it down to the mailbox Friday night and flipped the flag up so the carrier knew he had rare outgoing mail. Saturday morning, he'd been bleary-eyed from a sleepless night. While doing chores and chasing down his two pigs and repairing the fence they'd knocked down when they'd escaped, he wondered if he'd been a little too hasty in finalizing such a big decision.

He'd never known Malachi to be rude before. Or judgmental. Or, come to think of it, to look so stressed. Maybe he'd overreacted to his criticism. Josiah could certainly leave the impression he was frivolous. Even now, his new coworker was trying to balance a corn curl on his nose, much to the amusement of the remaining girls in the room. But Gideon knew Josiah was a quick learner and capable of quality work.

By the time he'd gotten the chores done, the pigs in, the fence repaired and was heading down the lane to retrieve his letter accepting the job and the move, the flag was down and it was gone. His steps had slowed to a stomach-hollowing halt. But like he wouldn't rescind his job offer to

Josiah, he wasn't going to rescind his acceptance to Bishop Brenneman. Although, for a moment, he considered racing up the lane to harness Jazz and chase the mailman down.

Still a bit sick to his stomach over the new direction his life was taking when he hadn't talked to Malachi and was leaving his brother in the lurch, he'd been subdued this morning at church. Making some excuse, he'd left shortly after the meal.

He didn't even want to think about the letter in terms of his feelings for Sarah. But knowing there were now only a number of opportunities to see her, he didn't want to miss one.

She'd been sitting at the table when he'd arrived. Though he hadn't spoken with her, his gaze had drifted in her direction all evening. He longed to ask to take her home. But to what avail? If he asked her to go with him and she didn't feel the way he did, she might be uncomfortable, making the last few weeks of working together difficult. Not a way he wanted to end years of friendship.

He'd told the bishop he could start shortly after the first of the year. That gave him a little more time to help Malachi out and let his brother hire his replacement. Besides, it was bad enough leaving. He couldn't imagine doing so right before Christmas when he might never see his family again. Even now, the thought soured his stomach like spoiled meat. And if he got the courage to risk their friendship and ask Sarah to go—and by some miracle, she felt the same way he did and said yes—it would break her heart and her family's heart to leave then as well.

Now that it was in motion, concerns he'd before downplayed about the move floated to the top like curds in cheese-making. Crook County, Wyoming, had 200-some Amish population as opposed to Columbia County, Wisconsin's 2000-some. He'd been looking for a less dense population. He might get more than he bargained for. Single women, any singles his age for that matter—which was something he should have asked the bishop about—could be in short supply. Heading West with a friend, companion... wife? might be a good idea. Gideon instinctively looked at Sarah. He winced. Was his happiness in leaving worth more than hers in staying with her family? With a sigh, he'd followed her smiling gaze on to the schoolteacher.

The schoolteacher, who didn't have community ties. At least not deep ones yet. Who'd already left her home and family and therefore might be willing to move again. Dorothy, who'd already smiled at him several times this evening. Sarah had wanted her new friend to have some attention. His? If he couldn't have Sarah, maybe he could please her by making her friend feel more welcome. The prospect didn't make his heart beat faster. He'd much rather have Sarah.

But as Sarah had said, her new friend was sweet. She was pretty. Gideon had gone out with girls for that alone before. It wasn't enough reason anymore. Maybe, if he got to know Dorothy better, he'd find she had other qualities. Maybe enough to prompt him to ask her to go West with him? Still, a moment later when he gave the blonde enough of an encouraging smile that she breezed over, it was because doing so would please Sarah. That was also why he asked to drive Dorothy home after a brief, but bland, conversation.

After that, there wasn't much purpose in staying. He would see Sarah tomorrow at work and if Malachi wasn't in the office, find some time and reason to talk with her there. And do that every day in the next few weeks so he could build a treasure of memories before he left Miller's Creek.

His gaze narrowed as Sarah flounced across the room after talking with Dorothy. It sharpened further when he realized her destination. He casually sauntered over to where Noah Reihl was standing outside a circle of other youth and bumped the young man in the side with his elbow.

"I thought you and your cousin weren't close anymore."

Noah scowled as he followed Gideon's gaze to where the dark-haired man smiled a little too wolfishly at Sarah. "We aren't. I certainly didn't invite him here tonight. But I could hardly tell the hosts to kick him out after he'd slithered his way inside." He shook his head as they both eyed the pair. "I wouldn't worry about Sarah, though. She's not foolish like some of the others who'd fall for his lines."

Gideon wasn't so sure. He compressed his lips as Noah's oily cousin watched Sarah walk away after a brief discussion. She disappeared into a downstairs bedroom just as Dorothy came out, tossing her cloak over her shoulders. The schoolteacher caught his gaze and gave him a demure smile.

Maybe it was time he got his coat too. He met Dorothy halfway across the room and dredged up an answering smile. "I'll meet you outside." Before she could respond, he continued to the bedroom and his coat. And Sarah.

She was sifting through the black cloaks on the bed. How the women could tell whose was whose among the similar garments, he'd never know. But, as he went to a rocker laden with blue work jackets and promptly fished out his, he figured they probably felt the same way about the men's coats. He jerked his arms into the sleeves as she pulled a cloak from the pile. She had yet to look his way.

"Are you riding home with Noah's cousin?" It erupted from him as an accusation.

"His name is Jared, and yes, he's offered me a ride home."

"I can take you." The words were gruffer than he'd intended.

She turned to face him and she flung the cloak over her shoulders. "Wouldn't that be a little crowded with Dorothy there? Or did you intend me to ride in the back seat while you canoodle in the front?"

"You wanted someone to make her feel welcome."

"*Ach, ja.* But it didn't have to be yo—" She bit off the word, looking as if she'd like to bite her tongue as well. "You're my friend, Gideon, not my brother or my beau. You can't dictate what I do."

"I'm offering a ride as a friend." Though his clenched fists and hammering heart wanted to say it was as a beau. "He doesn't have a good reputation."

"Don't worry. I can take care of myself." She swept from the room to leave Gideon staring after her with gritted teeth.

When he exited the house, Dorothy was waiting for him on the porch and Sarah was nowhere in sight. He scowled as an unfamiliar horse—one his horse-trading brother would have called flashy but a bad bargain—trotted across the farmyard and down the lane before turning in the direction of the Raber farm.

Half propelling a startled Dorothy across the yard to his own buggy, Gideon made fast work of bundling her into it. He pulled a buggy blanket from the back and made sure she had it all to herself. An extra one was folded on the leather seat between them. Just in case she told him she was cold and needed warming. It was a ploy that had been used before. One he usually enjoyed, encouraged and participated in. But not tonight. Tonight he was thinking that *Jared* better have enough blankets in his buggy to keep Sarah warm. His jaw tightened. But not too many.

"I'm so glad you asked to take me home, Gideon." In the dimness of the buggy's interior, the white oval of Dorothy's face was turned in his direction.

"Ja." At the end of the lane, Gideon looked down the road at the diminishing silhouette of the buggy and grimly turned Jazz in the opposite direction.

If she sat any farther over on the ragged buggy seat, she'd be hanging out the window. But at least she'd deterred Jared's invitation to *keep her warm.* Sarah didn't care if she arrived home a partial icicle as long as he stayed on his side of the seat. He hadn't offered a blanket and she wasn't about to ask for one. She just wanted to be home. And alone.

"Nice horse." She nodded toward the lumbering bay. "Looks fast."

"Oh, *ja.* Fastest one in my district."

I doubt it, considering his winging gait. Any horse that had the inefficient "throwing" motion of its front leg like this one was slower than one with a balanced trot. One like Gideon's mare, Jazz, for instance. Sarah clenched her teeth to keep them from chattering. "Really? I like to go fast."

"Do you?" He sent her a smile that made Sarah tug her cloak more closely about her. And not from cold.

"Ja. Open him up, let's see what he has." *And how fast he can get me home. Where I'll tell you a polite* guder nacht *and send you on your way. I never should have accepted this ride. And definitely shouldn't have gone looking for it.*

When the buggy lurched slightly forward at Jared's demand, she exhaled in relief. Home was only a few miles away. They'd be there soon. She wedged her shoulder into the corner of the seat and the door and tried to get comfortable for the duration, only to straighten up a short distance later when the horse slowed and turned into a tree-shadowed field road.

"What are you doing?"

Jared drew the winded horse to a stop, secured the lines and turned to her. "You're not going to ask me in, are you?"

"Unfortunately not." Sarah infused regret she didn't feel into her voice. "It's later than I thought and I have to get up early for work tomorrow."

"It's not that late. And a short night isn't bad if the reason for it is worthwhile."

Sarah knew she wouldn't like any reason he had in mind. *You were right, Gideon. I should have listened. But I'm only about a mile and a half from home. I can run that far if I have to.*

"All right. What might be worthwhile is getting to know you, Jared. How are you related to Noah?" Turning to face him as well, Sarah shifted so she perched on the edge of the seat. With her back to the door, she slid one hand behind her to work its way from under her cloak and search for the sliding door's handle.

He frowned at her. "Our grandfathers were brothers. But you're not interested in that." He slid closer across the seat.

Sarah frantically clawed for the handle. "Oh, yes, I am. My *daed* takes all his blacksmith work to Thomas Reihl. I didn't know his father had a brother."

Jared inched closer. "*I'm* not interested in that."

"I guess our interests differ then. *Gut* thing we found out now rather than later. Sorry you wasted your time bringing me home."

"I wouldn't say it was wasted. At least not yet."

His knee bumped Sarah's. She jerked hers away. His followed close behind to stay in contact. *Where was that handle!* Her breath escaped in a huff when her fingers finally bumped the cold metal. Wrapping her hand around it, she jerked the handle as hard as she could and prepared to tumble out backward if necessary.

Due to her odd angle, the door only slid back partially. Before she could shift to escape through the narrow opening, he grabbed her. Though she lunged away, he dragged her back into the buggy. After one startled shriek, she didn't waste her energy on the useless effort when they were too far from any farmhouse for someone to hear her.

She kicked and tried to beat against his chest. Those endeavors were also useless as her arms were tangled up in her enveloping cloak. Something he magnified by twisting it more tightly about her. He lowered his head to kiss her. She jerked hers to the side. Her hairpins dug into her scalp when he clamped a hand on the back of her *kapp* to hold her head still. Her frustrated scream was cut off when he crushed his mouth over hers. Sarah tried to wrench away. His grip was too tight. His other hand was maneuvering to find the opening in her cloak.

She was getting lightheaded when, with a sharp *screech*, the door behind her was yanked fully open.

Chapter Twelve

Sarah wheezed in a breath when Jared jerked his head up. Grimacing, he released his grasp of her head. When he pulled his arm past her face, she saw his elbow was gripped in a strong hand. One that quickly freed it to then wrap around her, cupping her shoulder and gently easing her back out of the buggy and against a broad chest.

Gideon. She wanted to sag against his supportive frame.

"You seem to have gotten a little lost, Jared. This isn't Sarah's home. I'll save you some time and give her a ride the rest of the way there." Gideon carefully shifted her so she was tucked at his side instead of between him and the buggy's scowling occupant.

Jared's horse flung its head up and sidled away when he yanked the lines free. "I don't know why I bothered to come over tonight. Your women leave a lot to be desired."

"I don't know either. Probably best that you don't waste your time anymore then. If Noah has any interest in seeing his cousins, he can go over to your district to do so. I'll tell him you're not coming to ours again." Gideon guided Sarah out of the way as the buggy was roughly backed out of the lane. He kept her at his side as they followed at a slower pace to where Jazz was parked along the road. He helped her into his own buggy, something she might normally have protested but much appreciated tonight when her legs felt like it might be the new year before they were fully steady again.

After a brief scan of her face, Gideon mutely tucked a blanket about her. The courtesy almost made her weep. As he walked around the buggy, she watched in the side mirror as the fluorescent orange triangle on the back of Jared's rig disappeared over a hill.

Her hands curled into her lap under the warmth of the blanket. Her chin dipped until it rested on her chest. Gideon had been right. He'd told her not to go with Jared. How was she ever to face him again?

The seat shifted slightly as he climbed into the buggy. She felt the weight of his gaze in the dark interior.

"You all right?"

From the way she slid farther down on the seat and pulled her knees up to lock her arms around them, he must've figured she wasn't. He leaned toward her and reached out a tentative hand, only to pull it back. "Did he hurt you?"

"Only my pride," she muttered into the blanket. "I should have listened to you."

Cold leather squeaked as Gideon eased back against the seat. "Now I know you're not all right." When she turned her head to eye him, he continued, "If you're admitting you should have listened to me."

"Oh, Gideon." Slipping her hands from beneath the blanket, Sarah slapped them to her burning cheeks. "I hate it when I'm so foolish."

She thought she heard him murmur something along the lines of "You're not the only one." But when she looked over, he was releasing the brake and urging Jazz into motion. To her surprise, instead of a fast road gear she knew the mare was capable of, the horse headed out at a brisk walk.

"Why—" Gideon's tone was conversational "—this time?"

Sarah furrowed her brow until she realized he was teasing that her foolishness wasn't a one-off event. She reached out to smack his shoulder but somehow the action became a single gentle pat before her hand disappeared under the warmth of the blanket again. Tipping her head against the back of the seat, she studied the shadowed buggy's roof as she pondered how to answer.

Because she was restless? It was true. Even with the enjoyable challenge of her new job, she'd been...unsettled lately.

Because she realized she could finally seek a beau, one with a future? Sarah quickly discarded the excuse. Gideon would know she'd never be truly interested in someone like Jared. What if he took that to mean she was looking in his direction for one? If she was embarrassed now, it would be nothing compared to how she'd feel if Gideon thought she was chasing him.

But that led to another possibility. She hadn't really wanted to go with Jared. And she wouldn't have. Until Dorothy came up, wiggling like a puppy with two tails, to share that Gideon was taking her home. Sarah scowled. She'd been foolish because she was jealous.

Something she'd never admit to him. But it did remind her of something. She twisted around to look into the empty back seat.

"Where's Dorothy?" He wouldn't have had time to take her friend home and get back to...rescue her.

Gideon grunted. "Josiah passed us on the way to her place. I waved him down and practically tossed her into his buggy. He didn't seem to mind. As for her? Well, if I was one of her students, I'd probably be writing on the chalkboard during recesses for the rest of the year." He flashed her a grin that slowly faded. "I was worried about you," he finished quietly.

With cause, apparently. If he hadn't arrived when he did... Squeezing her eyes shut, Sarah inhaled deeply at her close call. Gideon seemed to sense she didn't want to talk about it. She wasn't so much scared as...angry. Angry at herself for going when she hadn't really wanted to. Angry at Jared for being such a jerk. Even mildly angry at Noah for having such lousy relatives.

"In fact, instead of not seeming to mind, I think Josiah was quite pleased with the outcome. He seemed content to stay at the singing until we walked out the door. And he'd made sure we knew he was the one passing us. I don't think you need to look any further for finding Dorothy a beau."

Sarah sagged into the cushioned seat. She pulled the blanket up to her chin, not because she still felt so cold that she would never thaw out, but because the quilted flannel was soft—and had the lumber, varnish, hay, horse smell she associated with Gideon. Of course she was going to eventually relax after her incident. It had nothing to do with the fact that her pretty new friend's probable beau wasn't Gideon.

"That's nice," she murmured. "I'm happy for her." And she truly was. Although it would eventually leave her single again with everyone else getting married. The darker shapes of her homestead were visible in the distance. Sarah almost sighed in disappointment. It was so...pleasant here, with a full moon rising over the harvested fields, the cold now held at bay by the warm blanket, the steady, quiet *clip-clop* of Jazz's hooves on the blacktop. The comfort of her companion.

Sarah pursed her lips, wishing the buildings were diminishing in size instead of growing. The action made her aware her mouth was a little tender where Jared had mashed it against her teeth. She winced. *Definitely not the first kiss I've hoped for.* Surely not all kisses were like that? She was almost certain they weren't. When Aaron and Ben thought no one was watching, she'd seen them kiss her sisters-in-law much differently than what she'd just experienced. Simple, stolen kisses that she'd envied. As much as she'd dated, folks would be surprised that she'd never been kissed before. She snuck a look at Gideon and sighed. Folks would be surprised about a lot of things.

Gideon scowled faintly at the silhouette of the Raber barn that was growing with every stride of Jazz's long legs. He wished the farm was still a few miles away. He wished he had the courage to lift his arm along the back of the seat and if Sarah just happened to move a fraction of an inch in his direction, to nestle her against his side. He might, if it was any other girl. But it was Sarah. And she'd just been mauled.

He broke out in a cold sweat, knowing how different the outcome could have been. If he'd hurried Jazz like he'd been tempted to in taking Dorothy home, instead of holding the mare in check. If Josiah hadn't caught up with them so fast. If he hadn't used all of Jazz's speed once he'd turned in the direction the buggy with Sarah had gone. If the full moon hadn't revealed the rig tucked into the shadows of the tree-lined lane. He shuddered, drawing Sarah's attention.

"Cold?"

"Nee." Not hardly. If the fear of not having arrived in time didn't warm him, the honeysuckle scent of her hair when he'd held her against him did. And the knowledge she was only an arm's length away on a beautiful, quiet night.

If it wouldn't have raised questions and probably concerns, he'd have driven Jazz right past the end of her driveway. Instead, with a sigh, he turned the mare into the lane. "I guess I'll see you at work tomorrow."

"Ja." He tensed when Sarah put a hand on his arm. For sure and certain, she had no idea what it did to him when she touched him. "Speaking of work, you seemed upset on Friday. Is everything all right?"

No. Everything is far from all right. I need to talk to my brother after the way things were left on Friday. His stomach tightened. *I need to tell him I'm leaving the business and my family for what might be a fool's dream to go West. And leaving him, when even in his words, he needs me more than ever.* Gideon scrubbed a hand over his face. *I need to make sure Josiah is capable and gets up to speed quickly, to prove to Malachi my choice was a good one.* He darted a look at Sarah's concerned face. *I need to make sure I don't fall any further in love with you or I might never recover from my broken heart.*

He drew Jazz to a halt in front of the neat yard fence and stared at the porch of the well-maintained house. "I just wish this expansion was complete. I don't like…" *that I'm too much of a coward to really talk with my brother. That I'm too much of a coward to tell you how I truly feel.* "Where I'm at right now."

She rubbed her hand up and down the sleeve of his coat. The sight of her delicate, capable hand there and the slight pressure on his arm sent ripples up his spine. His heartbeat thudded in concert with his quickening breath.

"This too shall pass. If all the work Malachi is putting in is any indication, he'll have the new warehouse up and running before you know it."

Gideon gave Sarah a tight smile, slid his door open and bounded out of the buggy. Before he knew it? The words didn't bring any comfort. He knew a few things that would surprise and probably upset several folks in his life. Most immediately, Sarah. If he didn't keep her at arm's length in the next few minutes, she'd find them wrapped around her. Something she certainly didn't need after her recent experience. And something that could change their relationship, and depending on her response, maybe not for the better. Unfastening his jacket to the chilly night air, Gideon ran a hand across the back of his neck.

Sarah's brows furrowed as footfalls on gravel followed Gideon's trip around the back of the buggy. Something was definitely wrong. Before she could take action herself, the door beside her slid open and Gideon was offering her a hand down. He frowned when she just sat there looking at him.

"You sure you're all right? Do you want me to wait while you wake up your *mamm* or one of your sisters?"

Sarah shook her head. After the calm ride home, the episode with Jared in his buggy already seemed a distant memory. One to certainly learn from—*trust my instincts, don't let myself be goaded into anything.* One that, though it could have been a lot worse, at the moment only brought embarrassment. Ignoring his hand, she scrambled down herself to end standing in the narrow space between him and the buggy.

"I can't thank you enough, Gideon," she whispered.

He searched her face for a moment. Sarah found herself breathless, waiting for...something.

"What are friends for?" he muttered and took a step back.

Sarah's eyes widened. Whatever she'd been waiting for, it wasn't that. Sighing in disappointment, she looked over his shoulder and saw the dim lights of a buggy topping a hill in the distance. There should be little to no horse traffic heading their way this time of night. Gideon's offer to wake up one of her sisters made her eyes widen further.

"Oh, dear! I forgot to tell my siblings I had a ride home from the singing."

Gideon turned to look at the approaching buggy. "Looks like they figured it out. Or saw you leave."

Sarah worried her lower lip. "Still, I'm usually not so... irresponsible."

He swung back to face her. "Do you always have to be so responsible, Sarah?"

"Of course! It's very import...import..." she stammered under the intensity of his gaze. "Responsibility is a *gut* thing, isn't it?"

"I don't know." Gideon's voice was abnormally grim. "This is pretty irresponsible and it still seems like a pretty *gut* thing to me." Before she could do more than blink, he wrapped his arms about her and pulled her closer. His head descended, pausing a moment while his eyes searched hers, before his lips met hers. The whole experience was so lovely Sarah whimpered softly when Gideon lifted his head.

His arms immediately dropped away. He took a step back. Round-eyed, she stared at him. With a mutter, Gideon spun on his heel and briskly skirted the back of the buggy. The conveyance swayed on its wooden wheels when he launched himself inside. Sarah numbly retreated a step as, passenger door still open, the rig backed up and swiftly headed down the lane.

Motionless, she watched until it crested the hill her siblings had topped a short while ago. Her breath escaped in a quiet gust.

Now, that was what a first kiss—what any kiss—should be like.

Chapter Thirteen

"You're coming over to Miriam and Aaron's for Thanksgiving tomorrow, aren't you?" Ben looked up from where he was sweeping the sawdust from underneath a workbench.

Gideon grunted an agreement as, with a clatter, he tumbled the day's wooden remnants into the box they kept for anyone who wanted to take the scraps home. He wouldn't be going to Miriam's if he could help it. Spending the day with Malachi and Samuel and their families would have been bad enough. But unfortunately, Miriam—who was hosting the Raber meal as the senior Rabers had traveled to relatives in Minnesota for the holiday—had invited her three brothers to join them. So, now he had to sit across the table from not only Malachi, but Sarah as well.

Neither of whom he'd talked with in the three days since Sunday and…his big mistake.

Not talking hadn't been a problem with Malachi. His brother had rarely been in the building and when he was, Gideon made sure he was on the other side of the room or the wall.

But with Sarah…*ach*, it was hard. He'd almost chained himself to one of the sturdy legs of the workstations to keep from going in to see her. Though, whenever she'd opened the door from the showroom, he'd found some reason to duck his head. Still, all his senses had been focused on her.

The reasoning for evading both was easy. Guilt.

Guilt over not telling Malachi he was leaving. Leaving not only some vague time in the future, but in six short weeks. Just after Old Christmas on the sixth of January. Gideon tried to justify that at least he'd be helping his brother through the busy holiday season, but it wasn't much comfort.

There was no justification to soften his guilt with Sarah. He'd blown it.

He'd accosted her right after another man had mauled her. She could put both men in the same category as Gideon's continually escaping pigs and she'd be right. Gideon was so disgusted with himself that if he could figure out how to kick himself down the lane, he would.

It had been a mistake to kiss her. *Ja*, the full moon had played across her delicate features, causing him to marvel at her beauty. *Ja*, the fragrance of honeysuckle now almost made his head spin, like the few times in his early *rumspringa* when he foolishly attended big parties and had gotten a bit intoxicated. That moment Sunday night had seemed so…right. And for just an instant, he'd thought she was kissing him back. But when he lifted his head, instead of a pleased sigh, he'd heard a whimper.

He'd also managed to shock her into silence. Something he'd always thought near impossible with Sarah.

Ja. He'd blown it.

Ach, that resolved one thing. Now he knew she didn't want his kisses, so there was no point in sharing the depth of his feelings with her.

He grimaced. Probably just as well, with him leaving in six short weeks. But…oh, to at least have back their friendship. Yesterday he'd worked up the courage to step into the showroom and apologize. Only to find Sarah in a cozy conversation with that young *Englisch* wannabe doctor. He'd ground his teeth to the point he'd probably need dentures in the next few years. But the action had kept him from hollering that it was markup day in honor of the upcoming season and everything was four times the indicated price. And if you weren't buying, to get out of the store. Not the preferred action of a local manager. Maybe Malachi should question *his* hiring along with Josiah's.

Even with all the tool noise in the workshop, the men had looked up when the door between it and the showroom had rattled when it was slammed shut.

Gideon lifted a small nylon brush with a narrow wooden handle from a pegboard on the wall and strolled to the table saw, where he began brushing fine dust from the saw blade, the worm and the worm gear. Something that certainly didn't need done at closing time before a holiday.

So no, he didn't want to go to Miriam's and spend the day with Malachi and Sarah. But he was. His other option was to stay at home and dine alone on his dinner contribution, a variety of cheeses from the local cheese factory. The prospect was too close to what future holidays might look like for him after he moved away. Besides, his sister and sisters-in-law were persistent enough about family gatherings that they'd probably stop by his house and drag him out by the ear to join them. With or without his cheese.

At least Josiah seemed to be showing signs of working out this week. Except for Monday, when exuberance over taking the schoolteacher home the previous evening had him floating so high Gideon considered tying him down to keep the man from drifting up and getting stuck in the rafters. He'd scowled at Josiah to keep his mind on his work, unlike he was doing. To which the young man just grinned. Gideon kept both of them away from anything mechanical that day. But since that time, Josiah had shown considerable promise.

The adjoining door opened in the now quiet shop. Gideon tensed. He looked over his shoulder to see Sarah standing in the doorway.

"I'm closing up in here. Are you ready to go?" Her gaze flicked over him before she directed her question to Ben.

"Ja." Her brother grabbed his coat off the hook by the door. "Be right with you."

Sarah folded her arms over her chest as she turned back to Gideon.

"No." He shook his head and continued to brush vigorously, and blindly, at the accumulated sawdust. *I want to stay here and wallow. At least until you get your horses harnessed and leave.*

The door clicked shut behind the siblings. Gideon straightened to look around the dim and empty shop. It looked a lot like he felt.

Sarah strangled the dishcloth in her hands as she looked out the window. So he *was* coming. Heaving a breath, she resumed scrubbing the interior of a large pan. Dishes always multiplied when a feast was prepared. She didn't feel guilty about not cooking. Her sisters-in-law Miriam and Rachel were contributing, and Ruth and Gail Schrock were in firm control of the kitchen. Besides, dishwashers were always welcome. Sarah bore down on the cloth, scouring a stubborn stain from the pan used to cook the large turkey. She wasn't exactly hiding in the kitchen in case a certain someone showed up. Just doing a necessary job and taking her…frustrations out on unsuspecting dishes.

The someone was unhitching his mare and leading her into the barn where the horses of those who were staying awhile were stabled for the gathering. Did that mean he was going to stay awhile? On Monday morning, that prospect would have sent her over the moon. By Monday noon, when he hadn't stopped in the showroom, she still would have been thrilled. By Monday late afternoon, when she'd finally peeked into the workshop—after frequent hovering on her side of the door and willing it to open—and he'd studiously avoided her, her desire to see him had begun to fade like sidewalk chalk art in the rain. Apparently her kiss, one she'd remember all her life, didn't meet Gideon's experienced standards. Even now, her cheeks heated at the knowledge.

By Tuesday, she was ready with some snippy comment if he'd ever come through the door. He never did. Needing consolation, she went to lunch with Ben and Josiah instead of eating her sandwich in the office. When she returned from the Dew Drop restaurant, it was to discover that while she'd been gone, Gideon had been in the office, doing the paperwork he usually spent considerably more time on while he chatted with her. Later that day, eyeing his uncommonly neatly stacked work, she'd broken two pencil leads while recording sales figures.

By Wednesday, she was scared. What if he'd felt her response on what might have been just a joking kiss and realized that, given very little encouragement, she would flutter after him like every other single girl in their district and the surrounding ones? What if that affected their other relationship? Ruminating on the possibility, Sarah had paced so many times around the congested shop she was afraid she'd wear a trail. At least he didn't have to worry she'd show up at his house with a meatloaf or soup. But what if, by gaining a precious kiss to cherish, she'd lost something even more precious? His friendship.

Anne skipped into the kitchen. She'd been doing that lately since attending school. Adding a skip to her walk, a smile when talking. Sarah was very glad for her *schweschder*, but for some reason, the greater the groundwork of independence Anne exhibited, the more Sarah felt like little pebbles were falling away from her own foundation. At least in the last few days, Anne had finally shared her issues regarding the bully at school. Sarah had muttered that she'd say something to Dorothy to put a stop to it, but Anne had made her promise not to. Still, Sarah treasured the admission. She'd missed their closer relationship. Particularly in these last few days when she was afraid of losing her close one with Gideon.

"Gideon's here." When Sarah scowled at the announcement, Anne regarded her through narrowed eyes.

Sarah instantly modified her expression. "Did you get his coat and take it into the bedroom?"

"Of course."

At a lull in the general buzz of conversation in the other room, Gideon's voice floated into the kitchen. Sarah froze with a large pot in her hand.

"Did you two have a fight?"

Sarah jerked back to avoid the fountaining splash when the pot fell from her hand into the soapy water. "Of course not." She scrubbed fiercely at the residue where potatoes had briefly boiled over in the busy kitchen. "Why would you say that?" She added with studied nonchalance.

"Because you're acting strange." Anne pulled out a few surrounding drawers until she found one with dish towels. After selecting one, she reached up into the drainer and pulled down a pot that was almost a third of her size.

"I am not. And be careful," Sarah automatically cautioned as she extended a hand to assist her sister.

"I got it." Anne pulled the pot to her chest and awkwardly patted it dry before setting it on the counter beside her.

"I think we're ready." Ruth Schrock waited by the sink, ostensibly to wash her hands after carving the large turkey. "If you wouldn't mind carrying the serving dishes into the room…"

Sarah stepped away and dried her hands on the dish towel hanging on the handle of the oven, one wafting off heat from its busy use. She did mind. Carrying dishes to the other room meant seeing who was in there. Her mouth instantly dried up at the prospect of doing so. But she knew Ruth. The words were more a directive than a question. So Sarah grabbed the biggest bowl she could to hide behind and headed out to the numerous tables set up in the common room.

She almost stumbled when Ruth called from behind her. "Gideon! Would you come get the turkey, please!"

They met in the doorway. His gaze collided with hers. It briefly dropped to her lips before he looked away. But before he did, Sarah caught his faint grimace. She clutched the dressing bowl tightly for fear she'd drop it, just as her heart had dropped. Their shoulders bumped as they awkwardly passed in the doorway. The contact seared her arm almost as much as her hands heated from the warm dish she'd grabbed without pot holders.

She set the bowl on the closest table and backed away, preparing to disappear to…somewhere. Before she could, Anne, after depositing the bowl of broccoli salad she'd carried on the table, grabbed her arm.

"Sit by me."

As Ruth was indicating that all the dishes had been brought in to be passed around the various tables, Sarah did so, glad for Anne's preference of her. Something she regretted a short moment later when Anne grabbed another hand and requested the same thing. Her face flamed as she again met Gideon's gaze, this time over her sister's *kapped* head as they sat down at the table.

Her prayer, when Aaron signaled they should start their silent one before they ate, wasn't appropriate for any meal, much less a Thanksgiving one. The only thing related to the day was the desire to maybe see Gideon choke on the turkey's wishbone.

He needn't make it so apparent he regretted his kiss. That what to her had been a special moment was abhorrent to him. The reminder, and the possibility of losing his friendship over it, almost made her weep.

"Can I have the deviled eggs?" Sarah's fierce contemplation of her plate was broken when Anne bumped her arm.

"Oh! Of course." She reached for the platter and handed it to her sister, carefully adjusting her fingers so she didn't brush Gideon's as he supported the heavy plate from Anne's other side.

"I need your help," Anne mumbled over her first bite.

For the first time that day, Sarah's shoulders minutely relaxed. Anne rarely asked for help. Particularly lately. Sarah was still trying to atone for making her little sister back away from their previously tight-knit relationship. She set her fork down and shifted in her direction, struggling not to look beyond Anne's slight frame to the broad shoulders directly in view behind the little girl.

"I have a part in the Christmas program."

"Really? That's...that's *wunderbar*." Sarah bit down hard on her bottom lip. Anne had never done anything in public. The school Christmas program would be in front of the whole district. What if she got too scared with all the folks watching to say her part? She would only be embarrassed further. What had Dorothy been thinking to ask something like this of her sister so soon? Maybe she should have a talk with her friend. Ask her to wait until Anne was a little older...

"Lily convinced me to try for it."

"Oh." Sarah's narrowed gaze again met Gideon's, blaming him for the trouble his niece had surely gotten Anne in.

"*Ja.* I know I can memorize my lines." Anne slipped another deviled egg off the platter before it got away. "But our teacher said to practice them with someone watching so we get used to saying them while someone's looking at us."

"Oh! Well, for sure and certain, I can do that. We can practice upstairs before bed."

"*Nee.* The program is going to be on a stage, so everyone can see. I want to practice on a stage so it will be as real as possible. I was hoping a small one could be made in the barn and I could practice on it."

"Oh..." Sarah furrowed her brow. Ben or Aaron could make a stage. Even some of her younger brothers would be capable of something like that. Before she could volunteer one of them, Anne turned to Gideon and continued.

"I was hoping *you* would make it. You know a bit about working with wood. I only need a little one."

"Oh, we don't need to bother—"

Gideon's lips twitched as he nodded slightly. "I do know a bit about working with wood. I'd be glad to."

Anne nodded in satisfaction as she took another bite of deviled egg. "And I need you to watch me practice too."

"What!" Sarah's fork jerked, sprinkling broccoli salad over her plate.

"*Ja.* They'll be folks who aren't family watching the program. So I need to practice in front of folks who aren't family so I don't get nervous that night when they do."

Gideon set his fork down and rubbed a hand over his mouth. He eyed Sarah over Anne's head as the girl snuck another deviled egg before it left their table. "I suppose…"

Sarah almost shoved away from the table. "Then you don't need me," she muttered.

"*Ja.* I do." Anne frowned at her. "An audience of one isn't much of an audience. I need you both."

Chapter Fourteen

The Rabers' cow bawled its disapproval at the disruption of its normally quiet evening. Gideon smiled grimly as he deftly pounded the last few nails in to secure the final board of a six-inch-tall, four-foot-by-four-foot platform. Anne's stage.

He leaned back and swiped a hand across his brow. Though brisk late November weather seeped through the cracks of the barn, between the insulating hay and straw, the heat of the animals—with all but the cranky cow watching him with interest—and his exertion in building the stage as quickly as possible, he was warm. Or maybe the bead of sweat trickling down his spine was because Sarah would soon step through the barn door with her sister.

He'd managed to get through Thanksgiving day, though it hadn't gone as expected. Before he'd left for the gathering, he'd prepared to greet Sarah with a joking comment, something that would hopefully pave the way for his apology. But when he'd unexpectedly bumped into her in the doorway, what popped into his head was the memory of the last time he'd been that close. And the kiss that had followed. One he'd enjoyed—but she hadn't. And therefore, the immediate regret that he'd done it. The regret that not only hadn't he gained anything beyond the brief realization of a longing to kiss her, but he may have lost something precious. Her trust and friendship.

And he'd missed his chance to smooth things over and apologize.

Though he'd have preferred to sit far across the wide room from Sarah, he liked and wanted to support Anne, so he'd obediently sunk onto a nearby seat when the little girl had tugged on his arm. It hadn't taken long to realize they were being manipulated. He'd have been amused if Sarah hadn't been so upset. As soon as Anne had secured his and Sarah's commitment to help, the scamp had contentedly finished her dinner in silence. He'd turned from the two Raber siblings and, though he felt Sarah's glare—one hot enough to singe the hair on the back of his head—for the rest of the meal, he'd concentrated on catching up with Gail, his brother Samuel's wife.

Ben had asked Friday why he was carrying scrap lumber and a few tools out to his buggy. Gideon had replied that he wasn't sure he'd go to any more Raber-related meals if he'd known there'd be such a cost for attending. As for Sarah, she hadn't poked her head out of the showroom door yesterday and he hadn't poked his in.

But if Toffee's nicker, from where she stood watching in a nearby stall, was any indication, the creak of cold hinges and the chilly gust of air that followed announced her mistress's arrival. Gideon stiffened but didn't turn his head. A moment later, Anne trotted into view to step up on the small platform, a slip of paper grasped in her small hand.

"It's perfect."

"And all ready for you to practice your lines." He rose to his feet and stepped back out of the light from the lantern that hung on a rough wooden support beam nearby. Given the other member of the audience, it was better if he performed his duty from the shadows.

"If you pull a bale up and put it there—" Anne pointed right in front of the platform "—then you two can sit on it like folks will be sitting on benches at school that night."

From behind him, Gideon heard a hiss of indrawn breath. Apparently someone else had finally figured out where this was going. He cocked an eyebrow at the young girl on the platform. Anne smiled serenely back. Did this hip-high wannabe matchmaker think she could resolve the impasse between her sister and him when he, with his vast experience with women, could not?

Grimacing, Gideon turned to search for a bale—or two or three. His lips twitched when he heard the rustle of straw and returned with his first bale to see Sarah dragging one from the other side. When they had no less than four bales lined up, they sat down on the far ends, leaving a spot big enough to drive a team of lumber through the middle.

They sat there, him with his arms folded across his chest and Sarah, visible in his peripheral vision, with her white-knuckled hands clasped in her lap, while Anne practiced stepping up and down from the platform. Finally, she faced them and cleared her throat.

"Are we ready?"

Ready for this to be over. Gideon couldn't prevent a look toward Sarah's icy profile. He sighed and gave Anne a solemn nod. Regardless of the little girl's scheme, this wasn't going to work.

Sarah didn't feel the slight chill through her barn coat, nor the straw that poked her through her skirt and black stockings. Though she studiously ignored him, all her senses were focused on the solid, muscular form a few feet away. Someone who a week ago she'd have, without thought, been sitting right beside. Someone who a week ago she'd probably have caught the eye of and shared his smirk regarding this strange setup. Someone she'd probably have teased that he'd surely forgotten his lines at his Christmas programs years ago. It pained her dreadfully not to be able to do those things now.

Oh, to be able to go back a week and again have that relationship. To not have gotten jealous and accepted a foolish ride home with Jared. She might not have had Gideon's kiss, but at least she'd still have had his friendship. She sniffed. *My nose is prickling because it's cold in here, not for any other reason. I'm not going to cry.*

She'd seen Gideon arrive earlier and carry his materials into the barn. A week ago, she'd have rushed out to help him, or at least visit while he worked. Tonight, she'd dragged her feet leaving the house until Anne had grabbed her hand. She'd suggested several others to Anne for audience members in her place. Her sister had rejected all of them, adamantly repeating she needed only Sarah and one someone who wasn't a family member. As Anne was again confiding in and including her, Sarah couldn't deny her sister's request.

"The older kids will be telling the Nativity story. And some will be reciting the Beatitudes from the Sermon on the Mount. Then one of my new friends, Malinda, will be explaining JOY."

Sarah nodded slightly. Much of an Amish child's religious instruction came from mottos, like the constant reminder that *I* is the middle letter of pride. The emphasis on the word *JOY* was also a reminder to children.

"I have hers memorized already. *Jesus* is first," Anne began.

Sarah couldn't help mouthing the next, well-remembered

line, "*Others* are next." She heard Gideon's murmur join hers from the other side of the bales. "And *You* are last."

She couldn't help it. She smiled at him, amused but not surprised that though they'd attended school states apart, they'd learned the same mottos. When he returned the smile, so much tension seeped from her that she had to prop her hands behind her on the straw to keep from slumping off the bale.

"Then Timothy Hochstetler has his part. We share a verse. He has the first half. I have to stand close to him." Anne scowled. "He's already saying I'm going to forget my lines and sound as funny as I look."

Sarah jerked upright. She was halfway to her feet to wrap her arms around Anne and tell her sister she didn't have to do this when a gentle hand on the sleeve of her barn coat stopped her. Ten minutes ago, she would've jerked away, but at the pressure on her arm, she looked down at the tanned hand against the dark blue fabric and immediately stilled. Gideon, who'd slid closer across the golden straw, shook his head minutely.

"*Gut* thing we're here to help you practice, Anne. By the time the program arrives, you'll be so prepared, I imagine you could even say his lines."

Her sister smiled and looked at the slip of paper in her hand. "This has the first letters to help me remember. His starts with 'I must be a Christian child.'" Anne's lips moved as she concentrated on the paper. "Gentle…patient… meek…" She squeezed her eyes shut, obviously trying to remember. "And mild." She looked up at them. "It's funny because Timothy is none of those things."

Gideon tipped his head toward Sarah and murmured, "*Gut* thing I didn't have to recite that part of the old Amish school verse when I was young. I'd have been afraid *Gott* would smite me on the spot."

Sarah sucked in a breath, almost weeping at the teasing exchange. Something that would've made no impression a week ago was now a lifeline. She cleared her surprisingly thick throat and whispered back, "With what you must have been like as a child, He probably would have too."

Anne harrumphed for attention. "His goes on to say 'must be honest…simple…true.'" She sighed gustily. "Are you ready for my part?"

Gideon's hand still rested on the sleeve of her coat. Sarah remained motionless for fear he'd move it. And worse, slide back across the bales.

He lightly squeezed her arm and, to Sarah's disappointment, dropped his hand. She slowly exhaled when he remained where he was. "We're ready, Anne."

"All right. I have mine mostly memorized already." Anne straightened and primly gripped her hands together in front of her waist. "I must cheerfully obey, giving up my will…" Pausing, she squinted at the hayloft as if the words were written on the weathered boards there. "And way." She worried her bottom lip as her gaze dropped to her "audience."

"Well done, Anne." Gideon's voice, hearty with approval, rumbled from beside Sarah.

She smiled at her sister and nodded vigorously. Blinking rapidly, she swiped a tear that trickled down the edge of her nose with a knuckle. Who would have thought that seeing Anne on a homemade platform in a barn would elicit such a response? Maybe it was the spreading smile and shining eyes of her little sister. Or maybe it was the slight bump of the man's shoulder sitting beside her as he shifted on the bale. A casual brush that he might not have even felt. A simple touch that warmed her all the way to her toes because they were at least and at last talking with each other again. Something she'd previously taken for granted and now knew to be very precious. Even if it was just a start, it was still that. Maybe they could work back to the ease of their previous relationship. He may not care for her kiss, but at least she could still have his friendship.

"Get ready," Anne announced as she stepped off the platform. "We're going to do it again."

That was fine with Sarah. With Gideon beside her, she would happily sit on the rough bale all night.

Anne's lines were as smooth as a well-sanded and varnished table top by the time she was ready to quit for the evening. Gideon didn't mind if she practiced until chore time the next morning. It wasn't a Church Sunday. He could rest after his animals were taken care of. The barn was warm, the company...warmer. Had they really been able to regain their friendship? Even without his apology? Gideon sighed. It wasn't what he might once have hoped for while lying awake in the dark hours of the night, but their friendship was something he was glad to have in these next few weeks until he left.

During Anne's many recitations, Sarah had shifted so she was leaning lightly against his arm on their makeshift backless benches. Though his arm, braced by his hand on the rough straw, was falling asleep, Gideon had no plans to move it. This was a treasured connection, and a numb arm was a great improvement over the numb soul he'd felt for the past week.

But when Anne stepped off the stage and sagged to sit on the wooden platform, Sarah pushed to her feet. Gideon surreptitiously flexed his elbow to ease the prickles in his arm. Sarah went to the slumped little girl. Reaching out to

Anne, who clasped her extended hand, she pulled her sister upright.

"Time for bed. Past time for bed. You did *wunderbar*. You will be so ready when the program arrives." She directed a yawning Anne toward the barn door. As her sister shuffled in that direction, Sarah turned to Gideon with a smile.

"I wouldn't have said so Thursday, but I am really glad Anne insisted that an audience of one wasn't much of an audience. That she needed us both." Their gazes met and held. She inhaled softly and pressed her lips together. "I've missed you," she whispered a moment later.

Gideon knew what she meant. They'd been in the same building. Sat just a few feet apart at Thanksgiving dinner. But they might well have been miles instead of just feet and yards apart. "I've missed you too," he murmured.

And he was going to miss her a lot more. Because they *were* going to be miles apart. Hundreds of miles. It was time to stop dodging around the reality that he'd made a big change in his life. Time to tell someone he was going. Perhaps the one he was beginning to realize he'd miss most of all?

The hinges creaked as Anne opened the barn door and slipped out. Sarah tugged her bulky barn coat more tightly about her as the wind blew in. The cold air curled around him.

"I'm leaving."

Sarah headed for the open barn door. "Of course you are. We were out here much longer than I thought we'd be. Definitely longer than I wanted to be when I first came out." She grinned over her shoulder at him with the admission.

Gideon followed her. The difference between the warmth of the barn and the chilling wind blowing in through the open door almost made his eyes water. He inhaled slowly. "No. I'm leaving Miller's Creek."

Chapter Fifteen

Sarah spun back to stare at him. What she saw in his face must have confirmed he wasn't teasing. In the hollow at the neck of the oversize barn coat, her slender throat bobbed in a swallow. "What do you mean, you're leaving Miller's Creek."

It took Gideon a trio of slow breaths to get out what it had taken him months to disclose. "I mean I'm leaving." He pressed a hand against his stomach, which felt like it was dropping so far he'd have to retrieve it from his boots. "Miller's Creek. Wisconsin. I've accepted a position in a small district in Wyoming."

"Wyoming." He read her lips more than heard the word. Her eyes, in the paleness of her face, looked much darker than the blue he knew them to be. "Why? Why so far away? When are you leaving?"

His tongue felt glued to the roof of his dry mouth. "Right after Old Christmas."

Sarah slumped against the open barn door, slamming it shut. "So soon? Why didn't you tell me?"

"I'm telling you now."

Sarah left the door to return to the bales and sink down on the end one. Her elbows dropped to her knees. She buried her face in her hands. When Gideon trailed slowly after her, she jerked a corner of her apron from beneath the bulky coat and dabbed her cheeks with it. "How long have you known you were going?"

"I've known I wanted to for…a while. I only finalized that I was going this past weekend."

Gideon frowned as her hand fisted on the apron's fabric. He took a step toward her—wanting to offer comfort, wanting to hold her—before jerking to a halt. What if his comforting led to him leaking tears as well? Crossing his arms over his chest, he remained rooted.

"What did Malachi say when you told him?" Her mumble was directed to her lap.

"I haven't yet. I haven't told anyone in Miller's Creek. You're the first."

"Is it too late to…change your mind?"

"I gave my word to the bishop there."

"But…why? Don't you like it here?"

Gideon walked over to sit down on the far bale. "I do. I love…it here." And many of the people. "Sometimes you have to let go of something good to get something even better." The platitude, which had sounded encouraging to him in the weeks and months debating the move, now seemed flat and irritating. He sighed. "I love my brother and have learned a lot working for him. I'm glad I followed him here. But I want my own business. A small one. Just me and maybe one other."

"Couldn't you do that somewhere closer? There are new businesses springing up all the time. Maybe go as far as Green Lake?"

Gideon smiled faintly. Green Lake was the next county over. "I've always wanted to see… *Nee*, more than see, to experience, the West, Sarah. If I stay here, I'll always wonder about it." He shook his head. "And I'll always be under the shadow of my brothers. I'd like to see what I'm capable of."

"I know you're capable of whatever you set your mind to, Gideon."

He grunted. "Who knows? Maybe after a few months in a Wyoming winter, I'll be back with my tail between my legs."

She gave him a feeble smile. "It can't be much worse than a Wisconsin winter."

He pushed up from the bale and hefted it to return it to where he'd earlier gotten it from. He needed the physical action. He worked down the short row until he reached Sarah. Reaching out to take her unresisting hands, he pulled her to her feet. She looked up at him and squeezed his fingers.

"I'm so glad we've regained our friendship before you leave. I…" She drew in a shaky breath. "It would…break my heart to have lost it." Dropping his hands, she turned and hurried from the barn, leaving Gideon alone in the feeble lantern light.

Gideon stared down at the remaining bale. *Friendship*. Was he hoping she'd wanted something more? Probably, because right now, the word *friendship* just made him feel… empty. Leaving the bale in place—he had no more energy to lift it—he blew out the small flame with what felt like all his remaining breath and crossed the dark barn to the door. There was no sign of Sarah.

It was a cold ride home.

There was a quiet rumble of conversation in the lamp-lit schoolhouse. Sarah, sitting near the end of one long bench, smoothed the skirt she'd partially draped over the worn wood. Surely he was coming? She'd be so disap— *Ach*, Anne would be so disappointed if Gideon didn't after he'd joined them in a few more barn rehearsals over the last three weeks.

She craned her neck to look at the huddle of children, shepherded by Dorothy, in a front corner of the schoolhouse. Anne was there, whispering to her friend Lily. Surely he'd come. If not to see Anne, then to see Lily participate in the program.

A draft of cool air whipped past her black-stockinged legs, announcing another arrival. Sarah looked over her shoulder to see Emma and Thomas Reihl arrive and slide onto a back bench. Their granddaughter Cilla hurried along the wall to join her classmates. It seemed like the whole district was here. Gideon's brothers and their families, her older brothers and their families who'd come to see their younger siblings perform, Susannah and Jethro Weaver, to see her son Amos, Lydia and Jonah Lapp with their growing family, to see their niece Malinda Lehman, now daughter of Sarah's friend Grace, the previous schoolteacher, who was here with her new husband, Peter. Even the local EMT and his wife Hannah, who'd come to see their niece Lily participate, were sitting on the other side of the narrow aisle.

Everyone but Gideon.

Up front, the children were shifting into some semblance of order when the bench beside her creaked as someone settled abruptly onto it.

"I'm assuming this is for me. Otherwise you must have been eating all the community's cookies before they could get to the cookie exchange to need this much room."

Sarah could feel the cold air waft off Gideon's jacket. She tugged her skirt out from under him. Just like that, the lamplight seemed brighter, the crowded room less stifling, her heart a little lighter. "I was beginning to wonder if you were coming."

"I had to go almost all the way to Marcellon to find a place to park Jazz."

She smiled. Marcellon was a small town a few miles away. But the joke fell flat as she remembered that in just a few weeks, a little over two to be exact, Gideon would be going far more than a few miles away. Her smile faded, her fingers knotted together in her lap.

She'd stumbled into the house the night he'd told her. Thankfully Anne and the rest of the family had gone to bed. Knowing she wouldn't sleep for a while and not wanting to awaken anyone, she'd grabbed a lantern and crept down the basement stairs. There, among the jars of green beans and peaches and the earthy smell of the potato bin, she'd wept until she'd felt drained. Wept that he was leaving. Wept that he hadn't asked her to go with him.

Once she'd dried her tears, she determined to store up every possible moment with him. To save them as treasures to cherish later. Thank *Gott* they had regained their friendship to enjoy as she reluctantly watched the days march through the December calendar.

Though she'd caught a gaze or two from him that reminded her of the moment before he kissed her, Gideon never tried to do so again. She'd never admit to him the ache she felt when he didn't. But the kiss that had been so important to her now made her angry that it had driven them apart and wasted what was now precious time.

She'd never confess that she'd been praying his part of Wyoming had eight feet of snow this winter and extended sub-zero temperatures to chase him back to Wisconsin come spring.

The crowd hushed as the older children, including some of Sarah's siblings, filed onto the platform, one much larger than what Gideon had built for her sister. As Anne had described, the Nativity story was recited, as were the Beatitudes, along with other Amish homilies, before, with a collective and relieved sigh, the group left the stage.

Sarah pressed steepled hands to her mouth as Anne stepped onto the platform with the younger children. Her gaze narrowed on the boy beside her littlest sister. Terrible Timothy—as she'd privately dubbed him—didn't look so terrible. Smaller than she'd expected, he wasn't much bigger than Anne. His bowl-cut hair looked freshly trimmed, revealing a white border above the tanned skin of his neck and brow. His blue broadfall pants, clean but obviously handed down, were well-worn at the knees and frayed at the hem. As he took in the crowded room, his tanned face blanched to match the bordering white skin. Anne—though her face was solemn, her collar high and her sleeves pulled down to cover as much of her as possible—looked composed in comparison.

Sarah smiled as the meaning of Joy was recited. Knowing Anne was next, she gripped the edge of the thick wooden seat as Timothy shuffled forward. From her seat, she could see her sister behind him, waiting her turn. Except for the rustle of clothing as folks shifted on their hard seats, the room was quiet as they waited…and waited for Timothy's recitation.

"I… I m-must b-be a…" Timothy stammered to a stop, his previously pale face now bright red as he stared at the audience. After a moment, he blurted, "Christian child." Sarah furrowed her brow when he leaned slightly back. "Gentle. Patient. Meek. And mild." The words came in staccato gushes.

Sarah narrowed her gaze. Timothy's were not the only lips moving. Anne, standing right behind him, was mouthing the words a second before Timothy repeated them. The little boy took a deep breath, the next words still hesitant but heralded with more confidence.

"Must...be...honest...simple...true." Before the last word was out of his mouth, he dipped back into the line of the others. Sarah tensed, her grip tightening until her fingers ached as Anne stepped forward. She almost jumped when one hand was covered with a warm palm. Darting a look in Gideon's direction, she relaxed at his understanding smile. Releasing her punishing grip on the wood, she clasped his hand.

Anne's voice rang clearly in the crowded room. "I must cheerfully obey, giving up my will and way." As she stepped back into the line, Terrible Timothy gave her a smile. One that suggested Anne was now more his rescuer than his victim.

Sarah squeezed Gideon's hand and reluctantly let go as Dorothy came forward to conclude the program.

When it was over, Gideon rose to his feet beside Sarah. "She did well. I'm not surprised, though, with all the practice she had with her stand-in audience." He looked down at her with one of those looks that made her ache inside. "Do you want a ride home?"

An emphatic yes hovered on her lips, only to be squelched by the knowledge that Anne would want to share the evening's success with her. Torn, she worried her lower lip. She wanted the memories with Gideon, but when he left, the relationship with Anne—who needed her—would help fill the void. "I... I need to go home with Anne and the others."

Gideon smiled faintly and nodded. Already regretting her refusal, Sarah was glad the called greetings from the friends and neighbors passing down the aisle stemmed the awkwardness as they waited side by side for their turn to exit. Before they could step into the aisle, Anne slipped through the crowd and scooted into their row.

Sarah grabbed her sister's hands. "You were *wunderbar*!"

Anne's smile was almost as wide as the bench they'd been sitting on. "*Denki* for your help." Her bright gaze encompassed them both.

"Speaking of help, I don't think Timothy will give you any problems anymore." Gideon grinned. "You did well, little one."

"Ready to go?" Sarah glanced down their row to where her parents had been seated. They'd already exited on the opposite end of the bench and were making their way to the back of the schoolhouse.

Anne shook her head. "Miss Wagler has invited all us students to stay for cookies and hot chocolate." She bounced on her toes. "Then her friend Josiah and his brother will be driving us home in big sleighs."

"But I thought…" Sarah wrapped her arms across her stomach, one that suddenly felt hollow. "I thought you'd want to talk about the program…with me."

"We'll do that later. Right now, I'd rather be with my friends." Anne craned her neck toward the front when someone called her name. "I need to go. Bye!" She scurried back toward the front.

As she watched Anne join a trio of little girls, Sarah pressed a fist to trembling lips.

Chapter Sixteen

"Is the offer for a ride still open?"

"Of course." Gideon knew Sarah wouldn't want the community to know the depth of her hurt at Anne's rejection. He shifted to block her face from the passing throng. "But you have to walk to Marcellon with me to get Jazz."

"That sounds pretty *gut* to me. In fact, I wouldn't mind walking all the way to Madison right now." Ducking her head, she trailed him out of the schoolhouse.

"If that's your plan, you'll soon wish you had boots and a heavier coat."

They followed a well-packed path through foot-deep snow to where the buggies were parked. While he pulled a horse blanket from Jazz, Sarah went to find her folks and tell them of her plans. When she returned, she ignored his hand to climb unaided into the buggy. Frowning, Gideon climbed in on his side, retrieved a buggy blanket from the back and tossed it to her. With a grimace, she tucked it about her. They were on the road, with the steady *clip-clop* of Jazz's winter-shod hooves pulling them away from the school, before she spoke again.

"I thought she'd want to come home with me. To...to share her success."

"She is sharing her success. She's just doing it with friends who are feeling the same excitement that it's over and that it went well."

"But I used to be the one she always went to first."

Gideon looked over at her down bent head. "You wanted her to have friends, didn't you?"

"Ja." Sarah paused before mumbling, "But not ones that would replace me."

He reached over to take her hand. When she kept it buried in the blanket, he sighed and withdrew it. "They're not replacing you, Sarah. They're in addition to you."

"Ja. But I was always the one who took care of her. Ever since…" She hissed in a breath. "Well, ever since. She needs me." Her shoulders rounded as she hunched further into the blanket. "She needed me," she whispered.

Gideon rubbed the back of his neck as he stared through the storm front to Jazz's twitching ears. He smiled grimly. The mare was probably trying to figure out why, as they passed a few roads, he wasn't taking an active role in their journey. He didn't blame her. He just wasn't sure which direction to go himself. He ached to see Sarah hurting like this. How best to help her? A listening ear? A voice of dissent? He cast another look at her huddled form.

Dissent won. "Who really needs who more, Sarah?"

Her head jerked up and her mouth dropped open. "What did you say?"

"You heard me. Does Anne need you, or do *you* need Anne to need you?"

"I can't believe you said that." The blanket that had been pulled up to her chin was now jerked down to her lap. "Of course she needs me. I don't…" Her mouth snapped shut. When she mutely glared at him, he cocked an eyebrow in her direction. She whipped her head to stare out the storm front. "You're a great one to give advice on family relations. When are you going to tell your brother that you're leaving? You haven't yet, have you?"

Gideon winced as the barb struck home. No, he hadn't. Though there'd been no more closed-door meetings with Malachi, in the rare times his brother was at their location, it was obvious he was stressed. There hadn't been the right moment to tell him something that would add to his burden. Gideon justified that he'd gotten Malachi through the seasonal rush. All the holiday orders, even last-minute ones, had been shipped out on time. Historically, there was a little breathing room right after Christmas. Thankfully, Josiah was working out, though Malachi had never said another word about his hire either way.

Not telling weighed on him, but Gideon had shuffled that issue to the back of his mind as he dealt with other concerns as his departure rapidly approached. Preparing the property to sell—although an ache but not a worry as it would go fast, since houses with land were in short supply. Researching how to ship Jazz and the belongings he wanted to take, to Wyoming. Whereas his first attempt at making a buggy could be for himself, he wasn't going to risk not finding a good harness horse out there.

As he managed the shop and took care of numerous details needed to relocate cross-country, he searched every day for the courage to ask Sarah to go with him. When alone with her, the question would be on the tip of his tongue before he swallowed the words. In moments of selfishness, he prayed that *Gott* would provide the right moment to express them. But asking her might wreck the comradery they were enjoying. He couldn't bear having that distance between them again in his last few days in Miller's Creek.

Yet, here they were, side by side, when they might as well have been a mile apart. In the shadows of the buggy, he could see her stiff silhouette. Still, he couldn't regret his choice of pushing her a bit instead of simply offering a listening ear. Sarah, though stubborn, wasn't a fool. If he was leaving her, maybe he could at least leave her addressing a wound and starting to heal, even though she might hate him for it.

He sighed. "No, I haven't told him yet."

Sarah made no comment and turned away to look out the side window. Gideon urged Jazz to a faster pace to shorten the silent ride home.

Sarah sniffed as she hung her cloak on one of the pegs, many currently empty, by the door. A dim light and a few quiet sounds emanated from the kitchen. She followed them to find her *mamm*, who greeted her with a smile as she set up sourdough to proof overnight.

"I just got Wayne to bed. Your *daed* went up as well after taking care of the horse. I figured you *youngies* would be out a little longer."

Sarah pulled a chair out from the table and sat. It seemed strange to be in the house with only her parents and youngest brother. "I guess it will be a while before those in the program are home."

"Depends if they take their cookies and hot chocolate on the road with them. I saw a few sleighs, so that will shorten the time if they head in different directions."

"The *kinner* did a *gut* job tonight."

"*Ja*. For sure and certain, they did. The new schoolteacher is coming along very well."

"Anne did surprisingly well, didn't she?" Sarah looked up from where she was tracing the wooden grain of the tabletop with her finger in time to catch her mother's sharp glance.

"*Ja*. She did. Must have been all the practicing with you." Her *mamm* came over to pull out a chair across the table from Sarah and sit down. Though the oil lamp's flickering light cast shadows, Sarah could see her *mamm*'s usually cheerful face was solemn.

Gideon's words had stung. It had been too hard to face him after the thinking she'd done on the silent ride home, so she'd left him with barely a farewell when he'd dropped her off. Gideon might be a teaser, but she'd noted over the years he was also an astute judge of character. Had he been right to question hers? She cared deeply for her sister. But was there such a thing as being *too* attached to Anne?

She found another wood grain to trace. "Why did you let me stop cooking?" Though a whisper, it was loud in the otherwise silent kitchen. "Why did you let me pay her bills?" No need to identify who she was talking about.

Her *mamm* rested her clasped hands on the tabletop. "You saw the hospital envelopes when they came and dug them out of the desk. You cried and cried until you were sick, wanting to pay. We could have done without your money. What we couldn't afford, the community was more than willing to help. But you felt so terrible that we were ready to do anything that might help you heal. For a bit, we wondered if we'd lose you both." Her mom sighed. "I think in some ways, it's been harder for you to heal than it has been for Anne. Her scars were very painful, and as they're external, she'll face them every day of her life. We've—*you've*—ministered to those scars as much as possible. Your scars, ones of guilt—" she shook her head "—maybe we let them fester for too long. Maybe we should have been treating those as well. But it seemed to give you some peace to take over the care of her."

Her mom smiled sadly. "As for the cooking, the first time you saw a boiling pot on the stove after that…time in the kitchen, you vomited. I didn't want to put you through that, and well...it didn't make the rest of the family eager to come into the kitchen for supper. Everyone wanted to help you. So we rearranged chores." She reached across the table and gently rested her hand over where Sarah's restlessly traced the wood grain.

"I'm so sorry. We didn't know what to do. We were just glad to eventually have our daughters back."

Sarah rolled her hand to grasp her *mamm*'s. They sat quietly clasping hands in the flickering lamplight. A feeling, one Sarah didn't recognize, wavered just out of reach. Was it...peace?

At the faint jingle of sleigh bells, they looked toward the window.

Her mother smiled. "Sounds like our schoolchildren are home." She squeezed Sarah's hand. "Are you going to be all right?"

Sarah nodded slightly. "*Ja.*" Maybe eventually. But if she was going to have any chance to grasp the elusive peace, there was someone else she needed to talk with.

They both stood as the door burst open to an eruption of feet stomping off snow and a flurry of coats, hats and mittens being shed. A cacophony of voices called greetings, discussed the cold, touted the night's success and complained about going to bed, before the noise in the kitchen finally settled down again. Her *mamm* shooed the older ones out of the room and followed them after a final glance over her shoulder to where Sarah was helping Anne untangle her scarf from where it had gotten stuck in the pins of her *kapp*.

Once the scarf was freed, Sarah hung it on a wall peg. Sighing heavily, she worked up a smile before turning back to her sister. "Did you have a nice time tonight?"

"Oh, *ja*. It was much fun." The statement was tempered with a huge yawn.

"Did Terrib—Timothy give you any more problems?"

Anne giggled. "No. He wanted to sit by me in the sleigh. I didn't, because I wanted to sit with Lily and Malinda. But he said he'd share his lunch with me when school started again."

Sarah dropped her gaze to where a red line peeked from beyond the cuff of Anne's sleeve. "So, no more worries about…" she inhaled deeply "…your scars?"

Anne shrugged a slender shoulder. She shoved a sleeve up farther to contemplate one of the red ridges. "No. Lily says they're like her freckles, which she's had as long as she can remember. Just a part of her. And Malinda has something called a birthmark. It looks like one of the states on the map Miss Wagler has hanging on the wall. It's low on her hip. We had to go to the outhouse for her to show me."

"So you don't blame me…that you have the scars?" Sarah pressed her lips together to keep them from trembling while she waited for an answer.

Anne furrowed her brows. "Blame you? Why?"

"Because I was making supper when the soup spilled over you."

Her sister frowned. "Did you pour the soup on me?"

Sarah gasped. "Of course not. How could you ask that?"

"You never said and no one talks about how it happened. If you didn't pour it on me, then why would it be your fault?"

"You pulled it down from the stove. I wasn't in the room, but I was the one in charge at the time. I was responsible for you."

Anne's eyes narrowed as she considered that. "So, if someone's in charge and somebody does something they shouldn't, does that mean the person in charge is responsible for it?"

Sarah hesitated at Anne's shrewd expression. "It...depends. Why?"

"Leah kicks her clothes under the bed and doesn't dust there before *Mamm* inspects our rooms when we're told to clean them and Veronica doesn't get the eggs from under the black hen when it's her turn to do those chores because she's afraid of it. Sometimes those eggs get old and those are the ones that smell when you break them. Is *Mamm* responsible for those chores not being done right because she's in charge?"

Sarah's lips twitched at the tattling on some of their other sisters. "Not...exactly."

Anne frowned. "Then why are you responsible for something I did?"

Was forgiveness that simple? Sarah squeezed her eyes against the tears that rimmed them. She squatted and opened her arms. "Hug?" When Anne stepped into them and returned the embrace, it felt like an ocean of weight washed off her shoulders. Sarah leaned back and cupped Anne's shoulders. They didn't seem as fragile as the last time she'd done so. The action caused the neckline of her sister's dress to sag and reveal another scar.

"Do they still hurt?"

Anne shook her head. "Not that much anymore. They itch sometimes, but I can handle that." Her little mouth stretched in another jaw-cracking yawn.

Sarah stood and pointed Anne toward the kitchen door and on to the bedrooms. She couldn't resist a final squeeze of the slender shoulders before she let go. "I think you can handle anything."

Chapter Seventeen

"You were right. Again. But don't let it go to your head." It was the first time that day she'd had a chance to talk with Gideon. They were in the shed behind the shop, standing between Toffee and Jazz as they prepared to harness the mares. Everyone else had already left, scooting out as quickly as possible in case Malachi got back from the other location and changed his mind about closing at noon on Christmas Eve.

"About what, this time?"

Gideon's smile was tentative. Sarah couldn't blame him. Last night she'd subjected him to silent treatment. His words had hurt. Deeply. Probably because she realized how accurate they were. Because of her guilt, she'd needed Anne to need her. A salve for her penitence. Believing she was taking total responsibility for her sister—instead of lessening the remorse as she'd intended—had actually increased it. Last night's conversations had been a catalyst for change. She felt...lighter for the first time in years.

At least about her sister. The anvil now weighing on her was Gideon's departure in a few short weeks.

But today, with the bright sky and crisp but not cold weather, and Christmas in the offing, she had enthusiasm enough for both of them.

She ran a hand down Toffee's fluffy, winter-coated neck. "About my...tangled relationship with Anne. I had a talk with her...and my mother last night." She smiled. "It was *gut*."

Now he gave her a complete Gideon smile, one that lit his eyes and creased his lean cheeks. "I'm glad."

"For a long time, she *did* need me, what with *Mamm* taking care of the *boppeli* and everything else when I didn't for a while. But now...she's doing all right. She doesn't need me so much anymore. And I'm... I'm all right with that." Sarah grinned. The look that appeared in Gideon's eyes at her announcement made her shyly hunch a shoulder. She faked a grimace. "I suppose I need to thank you for encouraging her to go to school and introducing her to your niece. If I haven't already."

"You might have. But I'll let you do it again. Your two might help balance mine." His chest rose and fell on a sigh. "You're right. I need to tell my brother. No more delaying. And...thanks for not telling my news before I told anyone else."

"What are friends for?" Her lips twitched.

His gaze dropped to them. Sarah sucked in a breath and forgot to exhale.

She didn't blink when, with a jangle of halter and tie, Jazz jerked up her head. When that didn't get immediate attention, the high-strung mare swung her broad hips, knocking Gideon into Sarah. He caught her as she stumbled back into the more placid Toffee. The mares were tied too far apart for Jazz to cause any more trouble, but the knowledge didn't keep Sarah's heart from pounding as Gideon slowly lowered his head and his lips met hers.

Though seemingly impossible, it was even better than their first kiss. This time, it wasn't a shock. It was something she'd been waiting for all her life. In the midst of it, she even felt the earth moving, until she realized it was only Toffee shifting away from two people leaning against her side.

Lifting his head, Gideon apprehensively searched her widened eyes. She unconsciously tipped her chin up, inviting another kiss. He smiled and accommodated her. When Jazz stomped a hoof behind them, he met her gaze again.

"Is it too late," he murmured against her lips, "for a chance to be more than friends?"

"No..." Sarah regained her senses enough to give a tiny shake of her head. "It's never too late for that."

"Good. There's something I've been wanting to ask for a long time." His expression was somber. "Is it too late to ask you to go with me when I leave?"

Her breath left her in a gust. "To...Wyoming?"

He nodded slowly.

She swallowed hard. "As friends, to help you get moved in?"

He shook his head. "No, as my wife."

Sarah sagged back against Toffee. Exasperated with all the unusual activity, the mare reached around as far as the lead would allow and nudged her on the arm.

"I think I've known for a long time, Sarah. I just didn't know if you felt the same way. And I was afraid to ruin what we had if you didn't. But sometimes, you have to let go of something good to get something even better. I can't think of anything better than to have you permanently in my life. To have and to hold."

Her head was spinning. To be with Gideon. As his wife? Her heart pounded. Buried deep under layers of friendship she'd feared to disrupt, it was what she'd hoped for, longed for. Now that he'd opened the possibility of something beyond friendship, her longings responded to the warmth in his gaze like spring flowers responded to the warmth of the sun. Yes. Yes! Then she traced over what she'd just said. Wyoming. He was leaving. Saying yes meant leaving too. Her community, her county, her state. Her whole world. No! Anne needed her. What would her little sister do without her?

Sarah stared at him through a series of rapid breaths that gradually slowed. No, Anne didn't need her. Not anymore. Her little sister would do just fine. As would she, in starting a new life with Gideon.

"Yes," she whispered and watched his whole face light up.

By the time the horses were finally harnessed, Jazz was very impatient indeed.

Gideon slid sweaty palms down the front of his pants as he gazed at Malachi's new warehouse. He knew the majority of the work was being done on the inside, but even the exterior of the building looked considerably different from the last time he'd been here. Less…forlorn. Much revitalized. Now a building with potential. He studied it through narrowed eyes. He was beginning to see what his brother had seen in the old warehouse. He grimaced, regretting his intentional avoidance of the project and the particulars of its progress. Due, he reluctantly acknowledged, to his unspoken anger at Malachi for planning *his* life without getting *his* input on the matter. So much shared time and enthusiasm lost that could never be regained.

He exhaled heavily. He'd been dreading this conversation. Had put it off much longer than he should have. Just knowing it was there, in the back of his mind, had affected his relationship with Malachi. But, even as he reluctantly set a booted foot on the step, a smile lifted his lips. Now, knowing Sarah would be joining him, this task—though it still left a sour taste in his mouth and an ache in the back of his throat—was just a hard, necessary step toward their future.

He crossed the repaired landing to the door before looking back to see that Malachi's horse was Jazz's sole companion. His brother must have let everyone here off early as well. This was the time. No more delay. The new handle twisted easily under his trembling hand. He pushed the heavy door open and stepped inside.

When he'd visited the warehouse several weeks ago, the interior had been dim and dusty, the walls dingy, with debris lining the area alongside construction materials. Now, sunlight streamed through added skylights, the sealed concrete floor glistened and the white painted walls highlighted the organized work areas taking shape. Gideon momentarily forgot his dread as he strolled through the extended building, marveling at its transformation, until he located his brother in a small, makeshift cubicle used as an office.

Malachi looked up from papers scattered over the scarred desk and smiled when he saw him. "I didn't expect to see you here on a half day off, little brother. What a pleasure!" He looked like he meant it, which twisted Gideon's stomach more, due to the reason for his visit.

"*Ja.* You've...ah...the place is really coming along." Gideon's fingers were much colder than the comfortable air in the warehouse justified. Crossing his arms, he tucked them into his armpits. Malachi's smile faded at his solemn expression. He pulled out the chair behind him and sat down.

"Somehow, I don't think you've finally stopped by just to see what your new workplace will look like."

Under his palm, Gideon felt every beat of his heavy

heart. "N-no. My new workplace looks nothing like this." He inhaled shakily at Malachi's puzzled expression. "My new workplace is much smaller. Much more primitive. And is located in Crook County, Wyoming." He tried to swallow but couldn't get past the lump in his throat. "I—I'm leaving to apprentice and then take over a buggy-making business out there." Gideon exhaled harshly at finally, finally getting the words out. Lightheaded, he propped a shoulder against the wall.

Face so tense he feared it would crack, he waited for Malachi's response. The squeak of the desk chair ripped through the silence when his brother pushed up from it. Gideon watched warily as he crossed the short distance between them. He flinched when Malachi clasped his shoulder. "Congratulations, little brother. So you're leaving us to be a cowboy?"

Gideon shook his head. "Not a cowboy. But… I've always wanted to see the West."

"Now that you say that, I remember it from when you were a youngster."

"You're not mad?" He searched his brother's face.

"How could I be, when I've done the same thing? When does this apprenticeship in this new workplace start?"

"As soon as I can get out there." Gideon grimaced. "I'm leaving right after Old Christmas."

Malachi raised his eyebrows. His breath whistled from between pursed lips. "Afraid to tell me, were you?"

Gideon rolled his eyes and nodded vehemently.

Malachi stepped back to rest a hip on the edge of the desk. "I can't tell you how much I dreaded telling the folks when I was leaving. Especially when you two decided to join me. I thought for sure and certain, being a pacifist wouldn't stop *Mamm* from skinning my hide."

Gideon snorted. "Did you feel like you were going to throw up if you didn't pass out first?"

"Ja." Malachi smiled with comradery. "It was hard. Don't let it go to your head, but I'm proud of you, little brother." He winced. "I guess I can't call you that anymore, now that you'll be running your own business."

Gideon drew in what felt like the first full breath he'd taken in a long time. "I'm always glad to be your little brother. There's no one who I look up to more." His nose prickled. He pressed lips, ones slightly trembling, into a firm line. Sniffing, he blindly studied the polished concrete floor for a moment as he regained control of rampant emotions. "Probably why I feel so terrible leaving you in the midst of this expansion."

"We'll get through it. If need be, maybe Gail or Miriam can watch the *kinner* for a while and Ruth can come in and help. Anyone else at the shop you think could supervise until we move in here?"

Gideon lifted his head. "Ben. Easily."

Malachi nodded. "My thought too." He furrowed his brow. "Still makes us a man short."

Gideon frowned. He remembered the fallout on the previous employee he'd found. "You'll want to make your own hire."

"Nee. I trust your judgment. I must admit, you did pretty well the last time."

Gideon gazed at his brother's easy smile. His face felt hot and twitchy, like he could easily lose control of his expression. *Dear* Gott, *I'm going to miss him. And if I don't leave now, I'm going to embarrass myself by crying.* He straightened from the wall. "Thank you for making this easy on me."

"I love you. And I want you to be happy. I'll never regret the risk I took coming here. The move to Wisconsin brought me Ruth and the children. I'll always rejoice over that. I wish you the same."

"I'm glad, but I won't find a wife in Wyoming."

Malachi cocked his head. "You never know."

"Ah, I think I do. Because doing so would make the wife I'm taking out there extremely unhappy." At Malachi's slack-jawed expression, Gideon continued with a grin, relieved at being able to do so. "Sarah's going with me."

His brother slapped his hands together. "Took you long enough. I knew it was going that way a few years ago. But, *ach*—" Malachi shook his head wryly. "Now I'll need someone to replace her as well. You just keep putting me in a bind, little brother. Maybe I really will need to have Ruth come back for a while."

"If anyone can keep everyone in line and things organized, it's her."

"I'll let you break it to her tomorrow, when you come over for Christmas dinner."

Gideon shook his head with fake woe. "And it was going so well. You saved the worst for last, 'cause that's definitely the scariest part about telling you."

"You can handle it." Malachi pushed off the desk. "Come on. Let me give you a tour and show you what you're going to miss."

Gideon followed his brother through the warehouse, amazed and a bit envious regarding the future operation. But there was no question. What he was going to miss the most was the family he was leaving here.

Chapter Eighteen

Gideon double-checked the bit to ensure he had the right one before he inserted it into the router and wrenched it tight. After a joyous yet bittersweet occasion the previous day, he struggled to get his mind on work. He'd told his other siblings, Samuel and Miriam, about his plans, though he'd held back the news that Sarah would be joining him. He and Sarah, in order not to detract from Christmas, had agreed to wait for a few days to share that news further. After telling her parents this evening, they would talk with the deacon and request him to announce it next Church Sunday. Gideon smiled as he checked the pattern again. Waiting to tell his family was difficult. He wanted to share his exuberance that Sarah would be his wife.

This morning, he'd been able to tell—immediately—that Sarah had shared the news with at least one person. Based on the glare the usually reserved Ben gave him when he arrived at work, it was obvious that not only had she told her brother they were getting married, but that they were leaving too.

"You couldn't tell me yourself? Not as a friend? Or a co-worker? And you've known you were leaving all this time?" Ben's quiet reproach still burned in his ears.

Other than conversation absolutely necessary for business, his best friend hadn't spoken with him since. Not even when Gideon invited Ben to join him and Sarah in the office as they ate their bag lunches. Sarah apologized for telling her brother, but admitted she'd been so excited she needed to tell someone. Gideon totally understood, having shared the news with Malachi. Sarah assured him Ben wouldn't tell anyone and would come around. But apparently it wouldn't be anytime soon, as it was now getting later in the afternoon and Ben was still avoiding him.

Gideon sighed. Was this the way the rest of the community would receive the news? Not regarding his departure, but that he'd held off telling them for so long? Hopefully a wedding would soften the dismay, although there would be a few, previously hopeful, single women who'd be disgruntled. *Ach*, they'd soon find another bachelor on whom to bestow their culinary gifts. He grinned, something he couldn't seem to keep from doing since the episode in the shed. Would the district be surprised he and Sarah were finally making a match? Or would they be like Malachi, who'd apparently figured it all along?

He'd never imagined, when he hoped for the opportunity to express his feelings, that it would be, of all places, in a horse shed. But if *Gott* found a stable suitable enough for His son's birth, then it was surely appropriate for a proposal. After kissing Sarah and ascertaining her response, it had seemed the right moment to ask her.

He'd given Jazz an extra measure of grain that night. The mare had deserved it for literally shoving them together. Gideon now faced his departure with a much different feeling than he had a week, even a few days ago. It made all the difference, knowing Sarah would be there at his side.

Setting the bit depth to get the appropriate profile on an oak board that would become the front of a dresser drawer, he started his push-cut. As he moved the router through the oak against the bit rotation to carve out the design, his lips twitched as he realized the similarities. He was carving his own path in life, but much of the beauty of it—the solid oak—could be attributed to the sturdy foundation of his family.

He might soon be apart from them. But they'd always be a part of him.

Sarah turned as the bell jangled above the door to see a young *Englisch* man enter the shop. She smiled. It was the one she'd talked with about Anne. That seemed so long ago. The conversation had prompted Anne to attend school—making friends, gaining confidence, and ultimately not needing Sarah so much. Freeing her to be with Gideon. Given that conversation's results, Sarah was tempted to hug the man in thanks. Instead, she nodded in welcome.

He gave her a smile that would have warmed her if someone else's smiles hadn't built a fire she hoped was never banked. Her smile remained friendly, but neutral.

He seemed to understand, as his dimmed a few degrees as he approached. "Hi. I don't know if you remember me. Brad? From Madison? My mom bought a dining room set and hutch sometime before the holidays. I had a few days off over Christmas and came up to Cascade Mountain to ski with some friends."

Sarah nodded. She'd never been to the ski resort on the other side of Portage, but knew of a few *youngies* in their *rumspringa* who had.

"When Mom knew I was going to be in the area, she asked me to stop by. She loves her new dining room." Brad stopped across the counter from Sarah. "I can't recall if she mentioned that she's a real estate agent. She wondered if your shop would be interested in working out an arrangement to supply some furniture to stage new houses. There's a lot of growth in the Madison suburbs. As a big fan of your furniture, she thought an arrangement would work well for both parties. It would showcase your business to folks who might be looking to update their furniture when they move into a new house. She'd be happy to put out discreet cards detailing where the furniture came from."

Sarah raised her eyebrows. "That sounds like an interesting possibility. The owner isn't here right now, but his brother is. I'll see if he's available to come in and talk about it." Her pulse accelerated. Another opportunity to see Gideon. She couldn't get enough of them. Even though it had been two days since he'd proposed, she still had to pinch herself. It seemed surreal that their relationship had changed to something she'd been afraid to hope for. That she was going to marry her best friend. She thanked *Gott* continuously that Gideon had found the courage to voice his feelings. Ones she'd shared, but had been afraid to admit, even to herself.

She was less excited—much less—about leaving. Every time she remembered that aspect of her acceptance, her stomach dropped and her smile faded. Gideon had shown her letters from the bishop of their new community. One of which had included a few pages from the current owner of the buggy operation, describing the shop, the business and the home that would soon be theirs.

They'd leave shortly after the wedding. Sarah was counting with excitement the days until they married. With dread, the same ones until they departed.

As soon as she cracked the door, the noise of the shop spilled into the showroom. Sarah was surprised at the volume, as a few of the men had taken today off to extend their holiday. Swinging the door wider, she saw the three who were there—Gideon, Ben and Josiah, running machines at different stations. Her gaze automatically went to Gideon. Smiling, he turned off the router to tip his head inquiringly. She couldn't help grinning back before darting a glance past Josiah, who didn't look up from the table leg he was lathing, to her brother.

Bursting with excitement, she'd had to share her news with someone yesterday, so she'd told Ben, the sibling she'd always been closest to. Though happy for her and Gideon, he'd been more hurt than she expected by his friend not confiding the big news of the move to him earlier. Her smile quavered as she met his gaze when he looked up from where he was running a long board through the planer. She sighed in relief when he smiled faintly in return.

But the sigh was fragmented by a scream when, with a resounding crack, the long board split, kicked out of the planer and impaled her brother.

Gideon watched, stunned, as Sarah launched herself through the door. He spun to see Ben stagger back against the wall, a foot-and-a-half-long piece of board protruding from his midsection. Gideon sprinted toward his friend as Ben slid down the wall and onto the floor. Careening around a workbench, he slammed his hip on the corner and staggered a few steps before charging on. He fell to his knees beside Ben as Sarah slid to a halt next to him. Chest heaving, he stared at the red bloom on Ben's abdomen as it spread from the splintered wood. Heart pounding, he reached for the jagged spear.

"Don't pull it out!" The shout rang over the running machinery.

Gideon whipped his head toward the front of the shop.

An *Englischer* stood in the doorway. "Don't pull it out," the young man hollered again as he hurried forward. "Keep him and the wood as still as possible."

Gideon gaped at the intruder. Who was this man to be yelling directions? He'd seen him before but in the moment, didn't know or care where. In the next breath, Gideon jerked his hands back. The man was right. As a volunteer firefighter, he'd had training on this. Pulling the wood out would hurt Ben more. Still, his fingers twitched at Ben's long groan. He darted his attention back to his friend, who was pale and sweating. As Ben's hands reached for the piercing wood, Gideon grabbed his wrists.

"Sarah, go to the office and call 911."

The *Englischer* pulled a cell phone from his pocket, punched in some numbers and handed the phone to Sarah before she could race for the office. "Here."

She took it, and Gideon raised his voice for Josiah, not sure where his other coworker was. "Josiah! Grab the first aid kit. Also, there're microfiber towels in the cupboard next to the stain booth. Get me all the clean ones we have. We need to stop the bleeding."

The noise level dropped as machinery was turned off. "Got it!" rang from midway back in the shop.

"We need to control the bleeding. Unlike some other wounds, this isn't an injury you push on." The *Englischer* squatted beside Gideon. "I'm Brad, by the way. Move your hands to carefully stabilize the wood."

Gideon nodded abruptly in acknowledgement and did as instructed, gingerly grasping the ragged shard. He remembered where he'd seen the man. Weeks ago, flirting in the shop with Sarah. Hadn't she later said he was some sort of doctor? He seemed to know what he was doing. But could he trust him with his best friend's life? Sarah, her voice high-pitched and her face almost as pale as her brother's, related information to the dispatcher. Still, in their rural community, it could be several minutes or more before help arrived.

"What's his name?"

"B-Ben."

"Right. Ben, I know it hurts terribly. I know you want to pull it out. But it's best to leave it in until we get you to a hospital." Brad's voice had a calmness Gideon wished he felt.

Josiah, first aid kit in one hand and a stack of folded blue cloths crammed under his arm, skidded to a halt beside them. Brad took the cloths and began to pack them around the wound. Gideon hissed in a breath when the first ones immediately darkened.

"It looks scary, but the left lower abdomen is a recoverable injury. There's nothing vital there."

"Did you hear that, Ben? I always knew you were a man of good sense. Even getting injured, you do it in the right spot," Gideon hoarsely encouraged his friend.

Ben's eyes flickered open. "Hurrah," he panted. "But next time it's your turn."

"I'd take this one for you if I could." Gideon grimaced to control his emotions.

A control he almost lost when Ben met his gaze and murmured, "I know you would."

"Sarah." Again, the *Englischer*'s calm voice. "Any news on help?"

"They're coming. But it will be ten, fifteen minutes at best for the EMT." She'd bitten her lower lip so hard she'd drawn blood. "Twenty for the ambulance."

"All right. We need to keep the wood as still as possible. With the extra length, that will be difficult. Particularly when they go to move him." Brad glanced at Gideon. "Anyway you can shorten it while I stabilize it?"

Just the thought of cutting the protruding spear had Gideon breaking into a sweat. "Um." He swallowed. "Jigsaw. Probably work the best. We have a battery one."

Brad nodded. "We're going to ease him down a little further and slightly lift his feet. Keep a little more blood in the torso for the other organs."

"Josiah." Gideon continued his hold on the wood, keeping it motionless. "Get some boards."

"Don't raise them too much," Brad cautioned. "We don't want any abdomen pull."

Gideon never again wanted to live through those next moments, running a saw a short distance above his friend, who groaned and turned impossibly pale while the *Englischer* and Josiah stabilized the wood as best as possible. Sarah had swiveled away, a hand pressed to one ear, the phone to the other.

It seemed ages before Gabe, the local EMT, appeared, with the ambulance arriving a short time later. Nodding at the work that had been done, they quickly prepared and loaded Ben onto a gurney and whisked him away through the alley door.

Gideon stared down at the bloodstained cloths piled on the shop floor. He turned at the rapid footsteps approaching behind him. Sarah was there, her face as white as the *kapp* on her head. Her hands were twisted in the fabric of her blue skirt.

"Brad has offered to take me to Ben's house. I'll take care of the *kinner* while he takes Rachel to the hospital to be with Ben."

Gideon nodded. He ached to briefly hold her before she

left. A glance at his bloody hands stopped him. He curled them into fists.

Sarah pressed her hands to her cheeks. "What if I move away and something more happens to my family? I won't be there to help." She squeezed her eyes shut. Tears rolled from the corners to disappear under her palms. "They need me." She opened her eyes. They were as dark as obsidian. Or maybe that was just his soul, for he knew what was coming next.

"I can't marry you, Gideon."

Chapter Nineteen

"It wasn't your fault, you know. The wood split when the planer hit a knot. What were you going to do? Inspect every board that comes in and reject the ones with knots? Keep every tree from forming one?" Ruth Schrock shut the filing cabinet drawer and stared at him from across its top.

Gideon scowled at his sister-in-law and slumped back in his chair. It would be a long while before he could look at the floor beyond the planer and not see his friend lying there hurt. Probably why Malachi had closed the shop today. That, and the late night he, Josiah, Gideon and many in the community had, keeping vigil in the hospital last night. Local *Englischer* churches had loaned vans and drivers to transport several district members to Portage to support Rachel and other Rabers as they waited through Ben's surgery.

So it was just he and Ruth in the shop today. Ruth, because, with Ben now out and him leaving, she was preparing to come back to work for a while. Him, because he didn't know where else to go. He was too restless to stay home. He couldn't go to the hospital. Sarah was there. It hurt too much to see her.

"You don't have to be so…"

"What? Practical? Right?" She sat down in the chair behind the desk. "*Ja*. It's awful. No one saw it coming.

That's why they call them accidents." Her expression softened. "Praise *Gott* Ben came out of the surgery well." Her lips curved. "Last night at the hospital, I even heard a few praises mentioning your name. The grapevine says you made a difference yesterday. Responded well. Kept a cool head. Had Ben in position to transport as quickly as possible."

Gideon shrugged a shoulder. "It wasn't me. It was that *Englisch* doctor. He was the one directing."

"It takes good sense to know who to follow, and when to do so."

"I never thought I'd hear that from you."

"What?"

He cocked an eyebrow. "That I had sense."

"Well, you didn't have much when you first arrived."

They smirked at each other over the span of the desk. Gideon sighed. "I learned a lot from you. I wasn't sure I liked you. But I learned a lot from you. Then my brother had to go and marry you, and I had to like you because you were part of the family."

"Was that so hard to admit?" Ruth quipped in return. Apparently recognizing his teasing facade was only a thin sheath, she grew somber as well.

"I was going to leave, you know. After Malachi bought the business." At his expression, she continued. "Maybe you didn't know. *Ja*. Leave the shop, the community. Maybe even the culture, to follow what I thought was my dream."

He sat up straight. "Why didn't you go?"

Ruth tipped her head to examine the ceiling. "I think because I realized I wasn't so much running to something as running from something. My *daed* had died, the business had been sold. Many things I knew had changed. Seemed like a *gut* time for me to do some changing as well." She smiled. "Then I fell in love with your brother. Instead of running from something, I had something wonderful to run to."

"Any regrets that you stayed?"

"No. But that was my path. It's not necessarily the right one for you."

Gideon ran a hand over the back of his neck. "I don't know that I want to go now. Not when, for a *wunderbar* few days, I thought Sarah was going with me." He grimaced. "I suppose Malachi told you I asked her to marry me."

"He tells me a lot of things. But he didn't tell me that. Though I'm not surprised you two made a match of it."

Gideon launched to his feet and pivoted to face the wall. "Well, we didn't. Not anymore. She told me last night she couldn't marry me. Now I don't know what to do. I want to stay. Here, with her. But I gave my word to the bishop out there."

"Yesterday was a shock. She was upset. She might not have meant it."

"Sarah knows her mind." Gideon slowly exhaled. She'd put her life on hold for years because she'd believed her family needed her. Ben's injury had again triggered that internal tenet. Her family needed her. And that was more important to her than him needing her. He closed his eyes. Which he did, more than he could say.

"I don't know about Sarah. But if I were her, I wouldn't want you to stay."

Gideon's eyes popped open and he swung around to face Ruth. The words were like a slap to his face. It took almost more effort than he had to lift a corner of his mouth in a wry smile. "Now, why doesn't that surprise me."

Ruth leaned back in her chair and studied him. "Not why you think. I wouldn't. Because it would break my heart to have you give up your dreams for me. To have you, not always, not some of the time, but even just once in a while, wonder what might have been if only you'd made the move and tried it."

"She'd be enough. Our family would be enough."

"Yes. I believe you'd make them enough. But if I were her, I wouldn't want you to stay. I'd want you to go out and make square-wheeled buggies and freeze your ears off in a Wyoming winter. And then come back to me, just so you wouldn't wonder anymore."

Gideon smiled bleakly. "But what if I discover I like square-wheeled buggies and frozen ears?"

"By that time, I think I would have discovered that I'd be willing to give them a try too, just to be with you."

"Or found someone else locally. But you're not her." The back of Gideon's eyes burned as he stared at his sister-in-law. "I suppose I'm glad you're you, though." His shoulders lifted in a heavy sigh. "Take care of my brother."

"You know I will." Ruth smiled ruefully. "And the rest of them too."

Though the room's lights were off, the pale yellow walls reflected enough of the winter sun that was shining through the broad window to easily see her stitches. Sarah lifted her head from her knitting at the slight sound from the little machine on the pole by Ben's bed. She watched as, after a moment, the red numbers on it changed. Looking back at her knitting, she sighed. She'd lost track of where she was on the pattern again. Now she'd have to count back.

With her lack of concentration, she might as well have not brought it along when she came to spell Rachel. Her sister-in-law had been there all night and needed to go home to be with the children. Frowning, she backed out to the end of the row and shifted the knitting from her lap. Through the partially open door, she heard a murmur of voices and the tread of soft-soled shoes on the vinyl-tiled hallway. Though she waited, no one came in.

Sarah stood and tiptoed to the head of Ben's bed. Dressed in a hospital gown instead of his normal blue shirt and suspenders, with his quiet but alert eyes closed and alien tubes attached to his arms, he didn't look like her brother. She pressed her fingertips to her mouth. Rachel said he'd woken up a few times and though he'd been groggy after last evening's surgery, she'd spoken to him.

Sarah wished she could do so as well. She'd been so frightened when he'd been hurt. Thank *Gott* that between Brad and Gideon, they'd taken good care of him in those awful, awful moments until the ambulance arrived. Her fingers curled around the cool metal bed railing as she squeezed her eyes shut. *Oh, Gideon! I love you. But surely you understand that my family needs me.*

"I thought Rachel said that the surgery was successful. But you look like you're ready to lay me out in a pine casket." The words were slow and raspy.

Sarah's eyes flew open to meet her brother's half-mast gaze. "Oh, Ben! Oh. I'm so glad!" She reached out to grab his arm but jerked her hand back, afraid to touch him. Apparently understanding her intent, he leaned a hand against the railing. She grasped it, her grip gentle but grateful.

"Where's Rachel?"

"I'm spelling her for a while. She went home to be with the *kinner*. She'll be back later."

Ben nodded slightly. His eyes were open wider. He looked at the equipment beside the bed and the tubes protruding from him before gazing about the room. "How long am I in here for?"

"Rachel said the doctor said seven to fourteen days. You're on antibiotics and they've got a drain in to help reduce swelling from the surgery."

Ben dipped his chin in acknowledgment. "I need to get out in seven."

Sarah scowled. "You need to get out when they think you're well enough to release you."

"No, I need out in seven."

"Why?"

He furrowed his brows. "So I can be there for the wedding. I'm not going to miss my sister's and best friend's wedding."

Sarah's face froze. She carefully extracted her hand, pivoted to return to her chair, sat down and picked up her knitting. "There isn't going to be a wedding."

Wincing, Ben hissed in a breath as he shifted more upright in the bed. "What do you mean?"

Sarah jerked on the yarn, sending the ball tumbling across the vinyl tile. Though she grimaced, she ignored it, knitting stitches she knew would later need backing out. "It's pretty simple. We're not getting married. So there's no wedding."

She hunched her shoulders, anticipating a response. It was silent for a moment. She heard the sound indicating the machine on the pole was taking more measurements. She snuck a glance to see if they reflected Ben's mood at her news. They were only a few digits off the last reading.

"I must've been out longer than I thought. What happened? Just the other day, at least I think it was the other day, you were thrilled to be marrying him. While I, and the rest of the family when they find out, will be sad to see you go, I know they, like me, are thrilled to see you happy.

And you were. You were floating so high I thought you'd go up and out the chimney."

"You didn't look thrilled." She jabbed the needle into a stitch, splitting the yarn. It was quiet again as she knitted five—too tight—stitches.

"I was hurt Gideon didn't tell me earlier that he was leaving."

"Huh. He didn't tell Malachi until the day before Christmas. And he works for him."

She looked up to see Ben smile. "I guess I'll give him a pass, then. I feel better already."

"You asked what happened." She gestured toward the hospital bed with her needles. "Your accident did."

"What does that have to do with you not marrying Gideon? You surely don't think what happened to me was his fault?"

"Of course not. But how could I leave with him now, when you need me?"

Again, the silence. She finally shoved the knitting off her lap. She couldn't see it anyway through the tears that gathered in her eyes.

"Sarah, I'm going to be all right. This might have me down for a bit, but I'll be fine."

"*Ja.* But what if something else happens to someone in the family? I wouldn't be here. Not to help then, or later. I'd be hundreds of miles away."

"You're right, Sarah. Family is important. Now that I think about it, Gideon asked me months ago if I'd ever thought about leaving. At the time, I told him how *wunderbar* it is, with Aaron back, to have the family all together. How we all needed to be together."

"See?" Why was she even more heartbroken that Ben had just proven her point?

"What I see now is that in those moments when I was lying on the floor and didn't know what my future was, or if I had one, the ones I was thinking about were Rachel and my children. How blessed I've been to have them in my life. How I treasure every moment I've been able to have with them. I can't imagine a better man for you than Gideon. Family *is* important, Sarah. But the most important one is the one you create with the man you love. Which would you regret more? Going and missing us? Or staying and missing him?"

She held his gaze as tears splattered on the backs of the hands she clenched in her lap.

"I'll be out in seven days." He smiled. "Next time you come and sit with me, it might be good to work on a wedding dress instead of that poor knitting."

Chapter Twenty

Gideon heard the kitchen door open. He glanced out the window instinctively, but this room was in the back of the house and he couldn't see the hitching post from here. All he knew was that it wasn't an *Englischer,* as they would have knocked.

"I'm back here!" He straightened and considered the growing collection of items in the corner of the room, where he was preparing his things for the move. He should have asked the bishop the square footage of his new home. Thanks to the buggy maker's letters, he knew how many rooms it held. But there was a big difference between a house that was seven hundred square feet and one that was fifteen hundred. He shrugged, eyeing the items yet to be sorted. Well, he had the skills. If needed, he could make more furniture. His shoulders slumped. It wasn't as if he wouldn't have some long, lonely winter nights to do so.

Footsteps came to a stop in the doorway. Gideon turned to greet the arrival and almost sagged into a nearby rocker. Sarah was the last person he expected to see. Had she changed her mind? His heart rate surged. It continued accelerating as another, more likely reason arose. He'd heard his friend had awakened from surgery yesterday, but things could change in a hurry.

"Is Ben all right?" He tensed as a slight grimace crossed her face.

Sarah crossed her arms over her chest. "*Ja*. All right enough to act like a big brother."

What did that mean? Furrowing his brow, Gideon mirrored her position. He figured to visit Ben later today. Sometime when he could avoid the possibility of seeing Sarah. Leaving for a visit now seemed a pretty good idea.

She looked around the room. "What are you doing?"

"Someone's coming to look at the house. They might be interested in the furniture I don't take. So I'm determining the pieces that are going with me."

"Oh." Sarah worried her lower lip before nodding to the collection in the corner. "Is that what you're taking?"

"*Ja*. There are a few larger items too. The kitchen table and chairs, a bed and dresser, my Morris chair. These are just some odds and ends." He turned his back, reluctant to see her among the furniture he'd collected for their home.

He sighed as he viewed the rocking chair in front of him. It had been his first project after arriving in Miller's Creek. It was too delicate for him, but he'd made a few mistakes on it and Ruth had put up a fuss about selling it in the shop. To spite her, he'd bought it himself. Though the minor defects were visible, they weren't structural. As the years passed, he'd enjoyed seeing it in his home, imagining a wife who might use it to rock their little ones. Recently, it was Sarah he'd envisioned in it. His stomach clenched. *Ach*, he could always make another one if he should find someone out West. He shoved it to the side.

"What are you doing with it?"

"The new owners can have it." He narrowed his eyes at the rocker. "Or maybe I'll give it to Ben. He helped me a bit with it. Not the part with the mistakes. Maybe he wouldn't mind it as something to remember me by." He nudged the chair with his foot. It glided silently back and forth on its rockers.

"I'd like to have it."

At Sarah's quiet whisper behind him, Gideon spun to face her. Arms still crossed tightly over her chest, she met his gaze as she continually worried her lower lip. Obviously, she'd come to say goodbye. Not to tell him what he'd hoped when he first saw her in the doorway. That she'd changed her mind. That she'd go with him. That she'd be his wife. Could he stand to imagine her sitting in his chair? In someone else's house? Her belly rounded with someone else's child? *No*. He almost barked the word.

Then he thought of the times she'd sat in the chair when she and Ben used to visit. How well it had fit her. As if he'd made it for her. Maybe he had.

He nodded abruptly. "Take it." He marched over to unnecessarily scrutinize an end table. Behind him, he heard a few scuffles as she moved the chair. From the corner of his eye, he watched the doorway, ready to lend a hand if she needed his help getting the chair through it and out to her buggy. The scraping sounds continued, but she never appeared.

He turned to see her sliding it next to the items he'd determined to take with him.

"What are you doing? I gave that to you."

"I know. I'm packing it to go."

"But—"

"I imagine you're taking the bus. Do I go out with you, or do you want to ship me with the furniture?"

Gideon was lightheaded. He reminded himself to breathe. "Maybe I'll ship you out with Jazz. She'd probably like company for the trip."

"Then I'll make sure to bring horse treats along, and my own straw for bedding."

His lips twitched. He was afraid to smile. Afraid he was misunderstanding. "Are you serious? I don't want to drag you away from your family and into a...new adventure just because I'm ready for one."

Sarah solemnly held his gaze. Gideon's heart rate ratcheted up even as his stomach fell. She was still going to say no. She was going to back out. Why had he given her this chance to do so?

"I've lived an adventure that was something of my own making for the last several years. Anne did need me at first." Sarah paused as her eyes squeezed shut and her face contorted. Gideon wanted to fold her into his arms but a small sliver recognized that wasn't what she wanted at the moment. Instead, he crossed the room to gently touch her forearm and wait while she collected herself. When her face smoothed out, she offered him a smile, albeit a wobbly one, as her fingers wrapped around his. "I was trying to somehow make up for messing up her life before it hardly got started."

"We must be talking about a different girl, because Anne doesn't seem messed up at all to me."

"Nee." Sarah nodded. "She's pretty *wunderbar*, isn't she?"

"I think I know someone who might be somewhat responsible for that."

Her smile strengthened, though tears continued to trickle down her cheeks. With the hand not entwined with hers, Gideon reached up to carefully wipe one away. Before he could lower his hand, Sarah caught it and tenderly kissed his palm.

Gideon braced himself. If she was preparing to say goodbye, it was breaking his heart more than he could have ever imagined.

"So...as opposed to dragging me..." Sarah took a deep breath. "Intreat me not to leave thee, or to return from following after thee: for whither thou goest, I will go; and where thou lodgest, I will lodge."

Gideon exhaled in a gust at the words from the book of Ruth in the *Biewel*. Gently tugging Sarah against his chest, he wrapped his arms around her. She was laughing, even as more tears wet his shirt.

"I seem to be without an adventure at the moment. So I came up with a new one. I thought I'd try...cooking."

He gave an exaggerated sigh. "That might be an adventure for both of us."

"And as far as my family needing me, I think you need me more. To keep you out of trouble and protect you from single women in your new territory." She leaned back and met his gaze. "And to encourage you when you doubt yourself. And support and care for you when you work so hard proving yourself that you forget to do so. Face it. You need me."

"You're right. I do. And no matter my age or stage in life, I always will." He kissed her on the forehead. "We can see the deacon tonight. He can announce it tomorrow at church. Think you can put a wedding together in a week?"

She smiled at him. A smile he looked forward to seeing for the rest of his life.

"For sure and certain."

Epilogue

Gideon handed his new wife down from Malachi's buggy. His brother had driven them to the fast-food joint that served as Miller's Creek's bus stop. *It's the cold Wisconsin air stinging my eyes and nose. Not tears.* Either way, he sniffed as he watched the parking lot fill with buggies as folks came to see him and Sarah off.

They'd married in Malachi's new warehouse, decorated for the event, the day before Old Christmas. The timing gave Ben leeway in case his hospital stay extended beyond his self-determined seven days. His friend had looked gaunt but cheerful as he'd congratulated them. No one complained that the wedding landed on the day before Epiphany. Someone even commented it made sense to party and feast then, to fill up on the Dew Drop's cooking—who'd closed that day to cater the meal—as they'd be fasting until noon on Old Christmas anyway.

He tried to swallow past the thick lump in his throat when the silver bus pulled into the lot. The driver disembarked and, with Gideon's approval, stowed their bigger suitcases in the belly of the bus, leaving him and Sarah with a few carry-on items.

Sarah, smiling, but with a tear-streaked face, was saying her own goodbyes. Gideon turned to look at his siblings. Miriam had said her goodbyes earlier, not wanting to do so at the bus stop. Samuel and Malachi stepped forward, the hearty smiles on their faces not reflected in the blue eyes that matched his own. Gideon's ribs felt tight, like there wasn't room in them for the air he needed to get through this.

He cleared his throat. "I thought Old Christmas celebrated the arrival of the wise men. Not the departure."

"What are you saying? The wise men are staying. At least two of them." Samuel clasped him in a hug. "Take care out there. Let me know if they have any *gut* horses."

"If they do, are you going to come visit to check them out?"

Samuel's eyes were bright with unshed moisture as he clasped Gideon's shoulder before letting go. "Absolutely."

"Then I'll find some."

Samuel dropped back to wrap his arm around his wife's shoulder and Malachi stepped forward.

"*Denki* for the use of the building for the wedding."

"I can't think of a better start for it, little brother."

Gideon blinked to keep tears at bay. "I noticed the new sign."

Malachi smiled. "*Ja*. Well, I've run out of brothers working with me. Just plain Schrock Furniture can include Ruth and any of the children who want to join the business." He reached out a calloused hand. Gideon gripped it tightly. "It can also include a brother, if he ever wants to come back. He is always, *always*, welcome to return."

Nodding, lips pressed in a firm line, Gideon reluctantly let go.

"Make a good friend of the postman!" Ruth called.

Gideon waved. "We will." Packed snow crunched under their feet as he followed a tearstained Sarah to the bus and placed a foot on its lowest step. He paused there. And wavered. Though it wasn't where he'd spent his youth, Miller's Creek was where he'd grown up. It had been so good to him. How could he leave it? It was safe. It was known. For a moment he was tempted to tug at Sarah's cloak, whisk her off the bus and stay in the community's comforting midst.

He drew in a ragged breath. At the top of the steps, Sarah turned and looked down at him with a wobbling smile. As he met it with an equally trembling one, through a series of measured breaths, Gideon's galloping heart finally slowed. He climbed the rest of the steps to join her. He could do this. He could leave Miller's Creek for a new adventure. Only *Gott* knew what kind of adventure it would be. But Gideon knew who he was sharing it with. And that was more than enough.

* * * * *

Dear Reader,

I can't thank you enough for joining me on this journey! I set out to write one book about Miller's Creek. A few years later, this is book eleven of a fictional community that enthralls me almost as much as the delightful characters who have sprung from it. In the process, I've learned much about the Amish and the process of writing, along with a whole host of other things, including quilting. (I've made over twenty since the heroine in *Her Forbidden Amish Love* worked in a quilt shop!)

But the main thing I've learned is how wonderful Love Inspired readers are. Thank you so much for your support! To see what I might be up to (and if I've made more quilts) follow me on Facebook at https://www.facebook.com/authorJocelynMcClay/ or stop by my website at jocelynmcclay.com.

May God Bless You,
Jocelyn McClay

Get up to 4 Free Books!

**We'll send you 2 free books from each series you try
PLUS a free Mystery Gift.**

FREE Value Over $25

Both the **Love Inspired®** and **Love Inspired® Suspense** series feature compelling novels filled with inspirational romance, faith, forgiveness and hope.

YES! Please send me 2 FREE novels from the Love Inspired or Love Inspired Suspense series and my FREE gift (gift is worth about $10 retail). After receiving them, if I don't wish to receive any more books, I can return the shipping statement marked "cancel." If I don't cancel, I will receive 6 brand-new Love Inspired Larger-Print books or Love Inspired Suspense Larger-Print books every month and be billed just $7.19 each in the U.S. or $7.99 each in Canada. That is a savings of 20% off the cover price. It's quite a bargain! Shipping and handling is just 50¢ per book in the U.S. and $1.25 per book in Canada.* I understand that accepting the 2 free books and gift places me under no obligation to buy anything. I can always return a shipment and cancel at any time by calling the number below. The free books and gift are mine to keep no matter what I decide.

Choose one:
☐ **Love Inspired Larger-Print** (122/322 BPA G36Y)
☐ **Love Inspired Suspense Larger-Print** (107/307 BPA G36Y)
☐ **Or Try Both!** (122/322 & 107/307 BPA G36Z)

Name (please print)

Address   Apt. #

City   State/Province   Zip/Postal Code

Email: Please check this box ☐ if you would like to receive newsletters and promotional emails from Harlequin Enterprises ULC and its affiliates. You can unsubscribe anytime.

Mail to the Harlequin Reader Service:
IN U.S.A.: P.O. Box 1341, Buffalo, NY 14240-8531
IN CANADA: P.O. Box 603, Fort Erie, Ontario L2A 5X3

Want to explore our other series or interested in ebooks? **Visit www.ReaderService.com or call 1-800-873-8635.**

---

*Terms and prices subject to change without notice. Prices do not include sales taxes, which will be charged (if applicable) based on your state or country of residence. Canadian residents will be charged applicable taxes. Offer not valid in Quebec. This offer is limited to one order per household. Books received may not be as shown. Not valid for current subscribers to the Love Inspired or Love Inspired Suspense series. All orders subject to approval. Credit or debit balances in a customer's account(s) may be offset by any other outstanding balance owed by or to the customer. Please allow 4 to 6 weeks for delivery. Offer available while quantities last.

Your Privacy—Your information is being collected by Harlequin Enterprises ULC, operating as Harlequin Reader Service. For a complete summary of the information we collect, how we use this information and to whom it is disclosed, please visit our privacy notice located at https://corporate.harlequin.com/privacy-notice. Notice to California Residents – Under California law, you have specific rights to control and access your data. For more information on these rights and how to exercise them, visit https://corporate.harlequin.com/california-privacy. For additional information for residents of other U.S. states that provide their residents with certain rights with respect to personal data, visit https://corporate.harlequin.com/other-state-residents-privacy-rights/.